VENUS OF THE HALF

100 stories of exactly 500 words each

By Jim Marcus

. . . .

PULSEBLACK

Venus of the Half G

100 stories of exactly 500 words each

by Jim Marcus

July, 2024

This book is set in Lato Regular 9/13
Titles in Lato Heavy 16/20

Cover:
Venus of the Half G

by Jim Marcus 2023

Foreward by Ilker Yucel
Edited by Janet Valle

ISBN 979-8-9917282-0-1

This is dedicated to my children, Mission, Coda, and Donna, still the best stories I've ever had the chance to be a part of.

Index

Forward

Let's keep it short...
By Ilker Yucel

It is often said that art thrives in restriction, that when placed within clearly defined limits, the artist's creativity will explode in a deluge of orgasmic proportions... okay, perhaps not quite that dramatic, but there is certainly some truth in such a statement.

Barriers and rules are tested, perhaps even broken, the artist relying entirely on their ingenuity to create within those parameters, or to redefine and expand beyond them on their own terms, giving an almost impish satisfaction at having risen to the challenge.

More often than not, these restrictions are imposed, the artist's choice merely being whether to participate in the almost sadistic infringement of their freedom. It's a delightfully subversive notion to grant the artist an opportunity to be defiant and proudly say, "The rules do not apply, for they are meant to be broken."

Well, if anybody is familiar with subversion, it is Jim Marcus, for the spirit of rebellion seems encoded into his very DNA.

One could certainly describe him in the rather mundane terms of musician, painter, author, educator, philosopher – this would not do justice to the libertine and iconoclastic nature of his output... more accurately, he is a noisemaker, screaming with bloody, sweaty, tearful lungs against an obstructive society that almost aggressively revels in cultural and artistic uniformity.

Leave to him, thus, to mischievously turn the tables and place himself within the proverbial box of limitation, as he has done here with Venus of the Half G – 100 stories at exactly 500 words.

You might ask, "Why only 500 words, Jim? That can't possibly be adequate text to properly tell a compelling story, can it?"

Of course, he could give you the conventionally informative answer detailing his modus operandi... but what fun would that be?

And the fun does not end there, for aside from the restrictive word count, he has also imbued each of his stories with a time honored narrative device of the twist ending. No, not the superficial twist of simply hitting the reader with something unexpected for the sake of a surprised reaction, nor the moralistic twist that forebodes and enlightens, pompously granting the reader some greater wisdom... though they are arguably present within these myriad tales.

A temporal physicist consistently setting back the clock in an effort to breakup with a suicidal partner.

An Aeronautical expert attempting to solve why the physical laws of aerodynamics no longer seem to apply.

A budding young film writer whose romantic aspirations toward his fellow student seem limited to genre tropes.

A neurotic office drone obsessed with the square footage of his cubicle.

A lascivious sequel to W. W. Jacobs' timeless classic "The Monkey's Paw."

These are but a few of the strange scenarios that Jim has concocted to populate this collection and fuck with your mind, all masterfully confined to a word count so seemingly insignificant that the profundity of their narratives may leave readers with the bliss of literary post-coital satisfaction.

Here, allow me to light that cigarette for you.

Introduction

....

So, why doesn't the title count?
By Jim Marcus

In any enterprise, it's a good idea to have rules. And something I've discovered after years of parenting and over five decades of watching friends break laws is this:

People follow rules they believe in.

They break the rules they don't.

Some of you reading this are going to pretend to be shocked. We don't follow rules or laws for fear of punishment. We follow the ones we believe in.

The law in many states have traditionally handed down the same punishment for killing a cat as it has for buying a bag of marijuana. My guess is many readers have done the latter while most would find the former inconceivable.

You're likely shocked those two things might carry a similar punishment. If your cat is reading this along with you, you are probably acting even twice as shocked. For cats in this last situation, this probably delivers some troublesome insight into the affairs of humans and I'm sorry. To include you cats in this discussion, note that you all believe in no rules and follow none. Meow.

So there you go.

This is relevant because artists, musicians, writers, they need rules. They need genres and time limits and track limits and outside considerations to reign in the infinite possibilities of what they do. And sometimes it doesn't matter what the rules are, all that matters is that they exist.

And that you believe in them.

I made a conscious decision to write these stories, each of which is exactly 500 words, and each explores the narrative principle of anagnorisis. An Anagnorisis is the moment in a story where a character, or reader, makes a critical discovery that potentially changes the meaning of what's come before.

You can probably think of a number of books, stories, films, etc. where the ending is driven by this narrative function, where you, as a reader, or a character discovers something that makes them rethink the story up to that point. The goal is often to encourage people to think, to put down the book, and run the story through their mind one more time - to internalize the story. To possibly even internalize the rules.

And one of my rules is that the title doesn't count toward word count. Because I tend to think it would be cheating. It's not hard to write an expressive, absurd title to a specific number of words in order to patch up a story whose word count is wanting.

None of these rules are meant to get in the way of us having fun here. I appreciate so much friends who've read these stories and commented, friends who have tossed an idea my way, friends from whom I've stolen names, and those friends who have just been supportive. You are all amazing and too populous to name.

I hope that, with all that help, you might find this a worthwhile read, a place to go when you want to visit a tiny world with its own tiny rules.

1 - Able Communication

Ikadu stood motionless in front of the class of new students and tried to explain the excitement he had felt when he had first discovered he was eligible for learning the Korkori language years ago.

To the younger girl, his almost passionless intensity felt nearly as alien as the Korkori themselves, as she remembered seeing them on television during the treaty signing. She felt the importance of his words though, acutely aware of everything humans had gained in their newfound association with the Korkori, including the technology needed to build the water processing tubes arrayed behind this very building, sleek and futuristic, somehow accenting the organic lines of the rustic Hawaiian construction flawlessly.

Keani was so grateful for his visit to the class. His words had begun to put into perspective a lot of what she had been thinking over the last year. The sense of purpose growing inside of her was pulsing and alive and threatened to take over her entire presence, making her feel part of something big and important.

To punctuate his point, Ikadu broke into a perfect execution of the Korkori language, a complex dialect that required hand motions as well as gestures from the head and core along with the spoken sounds that came from the slim man's mouth. She instantly understood how his combination of neuro-divergent traits made him perfectly prepared to learn the complexities of the language.

So much so that it had become clear that the only humans expected to become fluent in Korkori were those with severe autism coupled with a set of physical obsessive compulsive tendencies - the combination that Ikadu expressed here.

And it was that fluency - that attention to the details of the language - that swayed the Korkori and made them into the staunch allies they had become. The aliens, advanced beyond our understanding, saw in us a kindred spirit as we expanded our understandings of what was "normal" and desirable across the neurospectrum. This work, begun years ago in classrooms and colleges, prepared us for a friendship that had grown into something beautiful and powerful.

A friendship that had almost instantly advanced humanity thousands of years.

A round of applause broke out in the classroom, filling it, wafting out the open windows into the near-tropical Hawaiian afternoon. The students in this particular classroom were already primed to think of today as a good day. Ikadu's visit only amplified this feeling, making him feel even more accomplished than he had when walking in the room.

Keani laughed a little and thought about the eighteen months it would take her to learn the unique emotional shifts of the Neramanki language. As she considered it now it didn't seem long at all.

She felt a spike in her normally high enthusiasm at the thought that only people like her had been able to navigate the joyful cadence of Neramanki and quietly gave thanks for the accident of birth that had given her Down's syndrome twenty two years ago, making this possible.

2 - Above the Earth, Below the Sky, is Ambercore, Where We can Fly

It's been thousands of years since the last war.

Thousands of years for humanity to decide, to determine voluntarily, what would be so important to them, in this new world, that it would take the place, forever and without fail, of anger.

Thousands of years for the people of this planet to learn to fly again over the battle scarred, irradiated earth below.

Thousands of years to invent, all over again, the ceremonies and rituals that would define us as human, in a world where it had become unthinkable that anyone would raise their hand to anyone else in violence.

Without the cruelty and animosity that had defined past generations, it was up to these new people to determine what defined them now, who they were. It was up to them to decide what fuel it was that made them burn brightly.

And brightly they did burn.

This new earth was filled with wonder, built by man, made to order to fill a new universe with possibility. Cities just like Ambercore floated thousands of feet above the ground, just as beautiful, just as magnificent, willfully defying gravity and providing support and protection to the millions of denizens of this new world, equal every one of them.

And on each of these floating cities, separate but connected via modern and equally magnificent modes of transport between them, unique rituals had evolved that gave each their own particular character.

We think of ritual as a remnant of the past and it's true, that is the role that ritual often fills. But, just as importantly, ritual can often stand as a symbol of our commitment to the future, as a living sign that we go on and carry with us the things that make us great. In this way, ritual is what we do when we believe, without doubt, that we will go on.

Ambercore was renowned for the way it had produced so many of this world's greatest scientists and thinkers, idealists and statesmen. The city itself represented aspiration, a commitment to being the best, impossibly, on a planet where just to look down was to see evidence of the worst man had to offer.

Here, on Ambercore, a unique ritual had evolved. One that embodied the philosophy of impossible greatness. Every generation, a volunteer from the Ambercore community, would put on the white robes of sacrifice, stand up on the tower that marked the edge of the city

And fly.

And each generation, the volunteer had, impossibly, stayed aloft for at least a few seconds longer than the one before. Until falling, inevitably, to their death thousands of feet below.

Seconds

If you peer through the early mist right there, you can see this generation's volunteer, white and fluid in the wind. You can see the people cheering her, excited, watches and clocks in their hands, waiting for the validation delivered by this ritual.

And if you listen, you can hear the people count as she throws herself into the wind.

3 - The Adversary

....

Maria wiped a bit of blood from her shirt and then immediately wondered why she bothered.

Most of what she could see was covered in blood, including the eviscerated corpses of most of her neighbors, ripped from their apartments and scattered across the searing hot hurricane of color outside.

She struggled to keep her thumb from shaking as she turned on the tiny voice recorder in her hand. Like most things in the apartment, it was Lisa's. Maria herself never really bothered to own much, except for a painting or two that used to be on the eastern wall of the building

When there was an eastern wall.

She began recording, "I don't know who will hear this, but I feel like I should explain."

And then she did.

Now, Maria is a scientist at heart and much of what followed was pretty dense. First, she tried to explain how Artificial Intelligence- guided art programs work.

AI art generators use a class of algorithms called generative adversarial networks. These algorithms are called "adversarial" because they have two opposing sides: One side is taught, and keeps learning, to generate random images; the other has been taught, and keeps learning, how to judge these images and make decisions about them.

Artists and programmers begin by feeding the input into them. Then continue by giving the program access to whatever other art is out there. So the programs can, technically, evolve and include new art styles, imagery, and icons.

That means, as humans create images and glyphs, figures, letters, words, visual blocks of things, that the AI can learn them and incorporate them. While the adversarial part tries to figure out which ones "work" best.

It was Lisa who had wondered if that extended to "magic words". She believed that some words, figures, and icons had special power, given them by the collective minds all around them - an idea that Maria thought was ridiculous. Until she opened the program and began to encourage it- prompt it to design the magic words for "Luck"

And everything changed. It began with Lisa winning that 20,000 dollars on a scratch off ticket- the ones she usually hid from Maria. They celebrated with the money. And that night, they found themselves closer than they had been in months.

But rather than focus on her good fortune, Maria began to wonder what else she was hiding. It took her almost an hour to generate the words for "finding the truth" and almost immediately, she regretted it. Lisa's tattoos were clearly visible in the pictures she found on her phone, accidentally sent by an unwitting partner.

The fight was conclusive.

After Lisa left, at 7:13 this morning, it took the computer, as directed by Maria herself, only 30 minutes to generate, over and over, the magic words for getting rid of sadness.

How could a scientist have known that magic words don't need to be read aloud?

And with a rush of superheated air, all sadness ended.

4 - Alive and Moving

It was entirely possible - probable, even - that this feeling - this compulsion, coupled with a pull, with a drive to move - was in his mind.

And that was understandable.

Some trips we make in our lives - our great Meccas- feel so inevitable they take on a bigger life in our imagination. We all get our purpose from somewhere, I guess.

And we learn, with time, to take purpose for what it is, with the understanding that it is often imperfect, open to introspection, flawed.

But it's still purpose.

He closed his eyes for an hour or so. If there were any better way to make it to Fallon, Nevada, he might have taken it. Despite outward appearances, and scruff notwithstanding, he was a wealthy man. He could have chartered his own plane and flown. Instead, through virtue of necessity he found himself one of twenty people on a tiny bus, moving toward the city.

Very slowly, it seemed. And, of the twenty or so people on the bus, maybe five of them were headed out to Fallon for the same reason.

To meet God.

Although it was entirely possible that was a bit hyperbolic.

But, to go all in on the hype, about twenty one days ago, a man in Fallon, Nevada had been conclusively proven to be Jesus Christ.

Not the reincarnation of Jesus Christ. Not some avatar or recreation of Jesus Christ. But the real, honest, and true Jesus Christ.

From DNA tests of the shroud of Turin to historical documentation, to carbon dating of his clothing, and twenty or thirty other tests, to the eerie grasp of ancient languages he possessed, this man seemed clearly to be the real deal.

And his discovery sent shock waves around the world. Or, it might have, if much of anyone cared anymore.

The man on the bus speeding toward Fallon might realistically be said to be one of the last of the believers.

If that weren't still sort of up in the air.

While the events in Fallon had triggered a small swath of new believers, if anything it had the opposite effect on him.

He rifled through the snack section at the oasis while the Bus refueled. A candy bar and one arcane flavored Mountain Dew later, he found himself back on the bus and moving once again.

He considered, in his head, what he might say to this ersatz Jesus Christ.

He thought about what proof he might ask of him, how he might make sense of the dilemma in front of him as he sat in the back of the bus and scratched at the scars in his palms.

Everything was becoming more real the closer he approached, more alive, more sensitive. And everything was becoming just a bit more confusing at the same time.

Of all the questions to ask, this was the one that drove him on. What do you say to Jesus Christ, when you know, for a fact, that you, yourself ARE Jesus Christ?

5 - All We Are is Numinous

Orocho had grown up in a home of worship, where images of the various gods peppered every room, building a sense of awe and wonder across his home. His mother taught him to be reverent and his father taught him to be bold in what he asked the gods for, understanding that these great ancestors would see his simple requests and proof of his faith in their power.

And, despite the fact that he had never felt closer to the Musubi- the energy that connected us all and created the cords that drew all people together, he sat in his hospital bed silent, without a single prayer in his head.

His mother had refused to visit him, ashamed. His father had rejected him and gone on to appoint his younger brother as the new head of his company. In 1984, it would be unseemly for any family to advertise a child dying alone of the GRID- Gay related Immune Disease.

And Orocho did feel alone.

Today would be one of his final days, if not THE final day. His fever hadn't been lower than 100 in weeks and the Kaposi's Sarcoma had turned his skin into hard, shell-like lumps, a suit of shameful armor.

Today, he would likely die.

He tried to imagine how he would pray to the Kami- the ancestors who had become gods in his beloved Shinto. He closed his eyes and thought of them, arrayed across the shinkai, watching and keeping vigilant over their people.

But Orocho didn't feel like he was part of that anymore. Whose people was he? He was a thing of shame, separate from the kannagara no michi in every way.

He remembered how his parents had reacted to Todd when he had introduced them, as though this shame was a permanent scar and he was no longer part of their line. The hospital he lied in today was like a living symbol of that shame, poor, antiquated, broken down. This hospital was a home for the unvisited.

Those who were now his people.

Orocho felt the tears slide down his cheek as he thought of them. He closed his eyes and tried to remember every one of his people here in this hospital, from the old man who had just passed away in the bed to his right, to the eighteen year old boy, so scared, crying every night in the room across the way. He gave each a name and placed each in his heart, and in doing so, the pain diminished.

As he leaned over and stepped from the bed, his feet felt light, sinking only slightly into the rarified air around the bed. He stood up, floating, and felt the wash of light across his newly deified body.

There were prayers in his head now, from all over the hospital, some unspoken, fervent, some penned in pain and the horror of this new disease. Orocho moved forward through the still morning light.

He would see to every one.

6 - And Now we are Four

....

Ilego had met the three of Charith's parents on Earth on their very first date.

The petite, reddish-hued Utangi girl had not wanted to hide anything from her human suitor. Not even the fact, documented in Wikipedia and available all over the net, that the Utangi had four discrete genders.

And Ilego had accepted all of that. He had even helped Charith's spore-partner, Dore, find work nearby so that they could maintain the close physical contact needed for everything that was happening today. And he had bonded, if you could call it that, with Foudio, Charith's wreath-mate, who had just arrived on Earth on a mining ship a week ago.

To Ilego, this all seemed to be moving so quickly. He knew, for a fact, without a shadow of a doubt, that he was in love. He absolutely knew it. But even in the midst of that powerful sense of purpose, he felt a vague unease. And had no idea where it was coming from.

He held onto Charith's hand tightly and stepped past the throng of protestors. There will always be people who don't understand, he thought, always, but he wished, on this one day, there were less visible.

As the shell-parent, Ilego had the honor of naming the child, and he had thought long and hard about that. The truth is, he seemed to think so much more clearly when Charith was around and that was when it came to him. Her name would be Hope. She would idealize everything great about the physical union of Humans and Utangi, and be a bridge to the future. Because of their starting configuration, he already knew she would be base-feminine, like Charith herself, but tradition held that she would resemble him a great deal. And that idea was more exciting to Ilego than he was willing to let on even to himself.

Ilego hadn't grown up thinking he'd even be a parent. And a lot of his closest friends had stepped away recently, acting as though his newfound parenting instincts were shocking or unusual. But in the back of his mind, ilego felt at peace. This must be what t felt like to grow up and finally put the needs of others ahead of your own.

But still, romance is complicated, and this one more than most. There were days when ilego couldn't even remember how he had met the Utangi triad that had become so very important to him. But then there were days like today, where a clarity and unity of focus made it clear to him exactly why he was doing what he was doing.

They all held hands as Hope began to claw her way through his abdomen. Ilego hadn't imagined it would hurt this much, but the calm faces of his partners seemed to act as a sedative, washing over him, reminding him why he was there and what the future held for this beautiful girl, under the loving tutelage of her three surviving parents.

7- The Artist

....

Ngedo Anansi's Punishment was supposed to have begun a while ago.

She waited in the shadow of the wolf to see if anyone would come notice her and reprimand her. But it had started to look, to her, like no one would come. It would be on the Elders' timeframe, not hers, that they would discuss what she had done and how they might end it. And this left her both giddy, prepared to jump up and speak in her own defense, and terrified of her own inability to explain to them why she had done it in the first place.

She turned off her senses and drifted for a bit, like a child might do on the river, or an otter, laid out on her back, her paw captured by another like paw, clinging to each other as their only way to direct their passage through the mysterious currents that professed to have no love for things like them in they way they moved- the way they jerked and flowed mercilessly toward any drop - any cliff.

There were a million reasons to be an artist, she thought, and each one, really more subversive than the next. Artists lived by a code to ceaselessly invent. It was the task of the artist to bring something into the universe that had never been, somehow, in some way. And Anansi had adhered to her responsibilities as an artist beyond measuring, beyond possibility, and, in the end, beyond common sense.

That would be their argument, she thought. It was an unassailable truth that she was umenzi, uzobe, umakhi. She was artist, maker, builder, as she had been since as long as anyone could remember. They would find no flaw in her commitment to making beautiful things. They would find no fault in that part of her heart, she was sure.

And she could pull from her boxes one after another, beautiful things that would counter any assault they might make on Anansi the artist.

They would call her crazy, unhooked from what is real, she thought, unable to make good decisions anymore. That would be the argument.

And each of the elders would look at her with that damnable grandeur, haughty, insufferably aloof, and they would do what they do to tricksters and artists time and time again.

They would look down and shake their heads. They would speak amongst themselves. They would point to her and vacantly pity her, pretending her mania was outside the scope of their understanding.

And this time, too, waiting, wearing her down, reminding her of her powerlessness - as the Elders had orchestrated.

Ngedo Anansi began to cry, thinking about these cold, unfeeling creatures destroying the beautiful things she had made.

She peered inside the world box and saw some of them now, staring into the void, defiant, chests out, exercising what Anansi had given them with every move they made, every action they took, enjoying the free will that made them so uniquely and uncompromisingly human.

8 - Assimilating

John had always called himself a futurist,

This wasn't an underground railroad. It wasn't some great sacrifice. It wasn't even a means to reclaim what was good in the world so much as it was just the future now.

The promise of the future.

He waited by the doorway for a taller woman to appear. She had long, curly hair and her makeup was flawless, barely covering up a look of fear in her eyes. John went over to her and hugged her, whispering in her ear the instructions on what to do next, where to go, how to behave. He pulled out a brightly colored dress for her to wear in order to escape notice and then laughed a bit under his breath as he noted it was nearly identical to the dress she was wearing.

She found it amusing as well, choosing to change anyway once she noticed, with a slight chuckle of her own that the one John proffered had pockets.

The two moved from the bright white space of the doorway enclosure to a neighboring cafe, lit in blues and greens from a giant fish-filled water tank, splashing movement and color across the metal and glass walls around the woman, causing her to stop and run her hands over each surface with the fascination of an artist caught within the bounds of a painting.

John listened to the woman in front of him, filtering out the specifics, trying to forget her name.

The doorway had delivered her here, four hundred years in the future, from a time where being transgender was a death sentence for so many.

He explained to her that she would need to stand up taller here, to not hide her height. She would need to be herself more joyfully, in order to fit into this new world that was every bit as expressive and welcoming to people like her as the world she left behind was toxic.

John was effulgent and silly. He joked loudly with the people at the next table and pulled the woman into his conversation. Her smile lit up as she joined in, assimilating easily into this new setting.

Now, so many transgender people had traveled here from the past that there was a risk to the timeline, one that caused many officials to consider an extradition agreement, sending them back if discovered, Even though it was a coherent effort to respect the timestream, John saw no enthusiasm for the idea, however.

He pulled himself away from his new friend, walking back to the enclosure.

As the doorway hummed to life once again, though, John noted in his head that while the extradition idea had driven his work underground, it had made nearly no difference in the day to day operation of his mission. Not today, when his clients assimilated so easily into this new world they had built, and not before, when he had first arrived here himself, tired and willfully waiting to discover his own future.

9 - The Astronaut

....

Waking up in an earth hospital was surprising to Rand.

And as he listened absently to the beautiful doctor to the right of his shallow and uncomfortable bed, he thought for a moment how he had gotten here.

Given his genetics, there weren't many options for Rand here on an increasingly volatile, fractious, and overwhelmed earth other than astronaut.

Oh, there was nothing necessarily wrong with him, nothing horrific. At 5'5" he was shorter than average. And his build, no matter how much work he might put into it, was never going to be grecian, for sure. Even now, his bit of a belly spilled out below his hospital scrubs, an outfit he was given, he thought, to clarify that he wasn't really a patient here, more a ward of the hospital.

Looking at the doctor, he saw, despite the dense severity of her words, what made her beautiful. And to her side, the nurse, with his own chiseled face and deeply blue, nearly purple eyes. Where Rand's hair had been desperately receding, as though on the run from some unseen assailant, since his late 20s, This nurse seemed to sport a head of hair that looked, and Rand really had no other phrases he could think of here, calmly content to just hug his beautiful head for all eternity.

He sat up in bed and was suddenly aware that he hadn't sat in a very long time. The last thing he remembered was being put into stasis, laying down, and placed on the conveyor ship. He and the other chosen astronauts would be the advance group that would prepare Alpha Centauri 3 for a full human population. He remembered actually being excited to go. This was a way for him to serve his people and help them escape the bondage of this wretched planet.

And it would have been easy. Many astronauts lived long and productive lives, clearing and terraforming, building habitats, cataloging animals, some even had the hope of being mainstreamed with the colonists once they arrived, to greet them, as a mentor, even, an expert on this strange world.

And that would have been Rand's life, If the conveyor ship's on board scanners hadn't caught that small t-cell abnormality. Tiny. Imperceptible. But it made him slightly more likely to carry disease and in a new world, that was unacceptable.

Every colonist was vital and each chosen for exceptional genetics and skills. To lose even one to disease was unthinkable. Especially when it could be managed and prevented so easily.

He took a deep breath. The room began to spin and then right itself.

Rand looked down, more than anything to spare the beautiful doctor the humiliation of having to look into his eyes as she recited, from memory, the planet's humble and enduring gratitude for his sacrifice and how being broken down to his component molecules in the food plants would be painless and easy and could he please check this box and place his initials here.

10 - Banned Books

Desato left the Rememory center with three tiny, unassuming silver pills between his fingers, at least one of which contained the obliteration of one of the greatest works in human history.

As he slid his butt along the microfiber softseat into the Freecar offered up by Glaxo-Smith-Kline and adorned with blue interconnected shapes advertising the ViagraMax, he wondered if there was any irony in the phallic shape and penetrative speed of the car under the weight of the external advertising and decided, definitively, that there was not.

This was his brain's job, he thought. To determine what was worth thinking about and what was not. And his brain liked its job.

As well, Desato loved the rememory pills that had become so commonplace. The idea of removing his favorite film from his memory and starting all over again, learning it, feeling it, for the first time, was hypnotic.

And all over the world, for many people, rememory was making the old new again.

The lights dimmed as the car lurched and threw him unexpectedly into the far door, causing a small bruise at the bottom of his spine. He called out in terror for just a second as the car righted itself and the lights chase back on. He had never seen an autocar, free or not, malfunction, and wondered what dilemma must have caused that. It was virtually impossible to confuse them.

Arriving home, he took a pull from the bottle of water on his desk and swallowed the pill marked for the great Gatsby. Desato took a deep breath and felt the book's plot dissolve in his head, leaving a space- a beautiful space to fill with a book he knew he would love.

And there were many like that.

Directing his attention to the white wall, Desato conjured up his stored list, books, events, and media that had created powerful good reactions in him and should be reread or revisited after their memory was removed. He smiled to see how many books he had sitting there, waiting for him, books he had decided he loved but he no longer had a memory of. Books waiting to be re-explored and loved again.

As he leaned back, though, he felt the tiny bruise on his backside from his narrow escape earlier that day.

It hurt

And it triggered some small amount of adrenaline. Not too much. Just enough to make him feel alive. To make him feel challenged by a world that had forgotten how to fight back.

He stared into the wall and, without thinking, flipped the list. In front of him now were 7 books and 4 movies listed that had affected him so badly, that had caused him so much trauma that he had chosen to ban them and unremember them. His eyes widened as they ran over the eleven items.

As the adrenaline thinned out in his bloodstream, he reached for his reader and chose the first of the eleven.

And he started to read.

11 - Breaking Up

Right as the bullet entered Ethan's mouth, tearing away the back of his head and splattering the eastern wall of the kitchen with a combination of blood, tiny bone fragments and brain-filled fibers from a black Affliction wool beanie, Grace considered how many times before today she had thought Ethan's predilection for dramatic acts of self-afflicted near-violence to be indulgent false machismo meant to control and narcissistically manage her own behavior toward him. So much so that it was hard for her not to say, under her breath,

"Well played, asshole."

She might have been more surprised if this hadn't been the fourth time she'd tried to break up with him and it hadn't ended exactly the same the previous three times. With a mental flourish, she scratched off timeline number 4 and reached down to the gaudy silver watch wrapped around her left hand, thumbing the chrome button to the left while the room spun itself backward two hours.

Ethan was back in his seat at the table now. Grace leaned back again against the stove and began her speech, this time approaching it from a different angle. Now she discussed her work, her research. She explained how close she was to a breakthrough, how her years as a theoretical temporal physicist had led her to a pivotal moment, one that required all her attention. And as much as she had appreciated Ethan's lust for life and guitar-solo-heavy late night household distractions, she needed to focus now and to do that, she needed to be alone.

The speech flowed seamlessly from Grace's mouth while Ethan fumed, suddenly turning to the kitchen drawer to his right and snatching a different gun. Grace began to wonder how many of those were scattered about the house as Ethan raged about his fantasies of betrayal and loss. And then, in a moment of pique represented through a wild flailing of arms, Ethan pretended to be in radical danger of killing himself as his antics caused him to perforate his skull with a bullet.

Again.

After having seen Ethan accidentally murder himself five times in a row attempting to coerce her into staying, Grace felt an overwhelming wash of emotion, not the least of which was the internal affirmation of her initial instincts to break up with this microcephallic idiot, followed closely by the sadness rendered by her lack of inspiration to do it last week.

And that's when it occurred to Grace that she needed to choose her time better, moving backwards to last week when Ethan, cheerful and full of life from the most recent concert he had seen, would possibly be more capable of responding in an adult way.

"A cheerful Ethan would be easier to talk to."

And 17 minutes later, those were still the words echoing through her head while the bullet ripped through her chest, propelled by the weapon in Ethan's sweaty hand, his mouth denying having done anything while Grace felt herself disappear for the last time.

12 - The Bucket

Looking down at the cedarwood floor of the back porch, stained rust red with blood, Selina sighed. She eased herself down to a kneeling position and started to scrub, listening for the creaking of the old timbers that she had been warned about over her own various creaks and groans.

But she heard nothing. People in Selina's generation were generally not enamored of ghosts. In fact, hers was the generation most terrified, most afraid that some half-remembered nemesis might die en route to telling them off and fail to realize, as they reached their destination, that they had died in transit. And now could do nothing but haunt the inhabitants.

Ghosts were always a reality, a possibility, albeit a distant one. And houses like this were almost meant to carry ghosts along with them, like rats on giant wooden ships – unwanted stowaways that made their presence known when it was least wanted.

The water in front of her was deep red by the time the slats of porchwood were clean, sloshing within the bucket, threatening to spill out across the floor with every one of her lurching movements. Selina was tired and this house would likely suck up the last of her remaining energy.

The story she had heard, somewhere, although she couldn't remember exactly where, was that a child was killed here, causing that beloved child's caretaker to commit the worst act that the home itself could imagine. She took her own life. And against the screams of the home, the power of its own rejection of her act, that caretaker died, confused and wanting.

And this house took that soul for its own use

But Selina was a woman of purpose, one who considered herself modern and even attached to the modern sciences. She was not easily spooked or swayed by talk of ghosts and demons and the like.

In fact, once she had had the chance to clean this place up to her standards, she suspected that it would be much harder to imagine a panoply of spooks and spectres moving through its arteries like blood cells, bringing a kind of anti-life to this old structure.

It would be, she hoped, harder to conceive of this home as some shell for sysyphean half-people, going about their pre-recorded lives as though trapped in some endless tape loop, performing again and again, meaningless tasks that might one day assuage their conscience enough to go to a better place.

She smiled as she continued her walk through of the house. In fact, it would be a charming, light and lively home for children again. A place where they might thrive and grow. That would be nice

Walking past the kitchen she spied the rust red blood splatter across the porch's cedarwood floor. She picked up the bucket near the door, filled with clean soapy water and sighed. Easing herself down to a kneeling position, she began to scrub, listening for the expected creaking of the old timbers.

She heard nothing.

13 - By the Red Light of the Revolution

It was the wantonness of the murders that should have been the first clue-how the colonists killed the natives in patterns, idealized shapes, all over the country, killed when they could have easily gotten what they wanted otherwise, destroyed where they could have shared, Defiled and maimed where they could have quite easily convinced.

When treaties were signed and good men drank together, only to find their families cut to pieces in the morning, hanging oddly, bleeding out amongst strange sigils carved in the first below them, or etched on trees all around them.

Yes, this was a clue.

The inhumanity of it all wasn't accidental. And the enslaved ones they imported, these died, not like cattle or even objects of use, workers that had value. They didn't die like goods that brought resources at auction, whose labor in the fields kept entire states alive and prosperous.

No, these, too, died ritualistically, without surface meaning, in ways that were often mysterious and challenging to observers.

If there were any.

These died sacrificially, as servants to the pyramids of their masters, bound by the faddish will of priests and conjurers. They died connected to history by the thin thread of magic, where pharaohs and fanaticists invoked futures that aligned with their needs and commanded forces beyond them to get there.

Futures we lived in.

Since the beginning of time, these should have been the signs. This should have been notification to the world that they were watching the birth of something bigger- a warning to stand back, perhaps.

Death has been a tool for centuries, not just to cow and steal, but to speak to the otherworldly forces that have, consistently, ignored the pleas of man, again and again otherwise. In a world where each side of every conflict invokes God and their own rectitude in his eyes, it's the side most willing to send him a calf or two, slaughtered without regret, fresh from the table, that gains his ear.

And these Americans were wise. Like their Benjamin Franklin, whose mind, expanded through use of the herbs and wild mushrooms available in this new world, was able to plot futures through any means at his disposal, both scientific, and mystical, worldly and...

Well, more.

And this George Washington, whose sacrificial adornment of teeth from the bodies of the enslaved, extracted through the tightest requirements, made him virtually unstoppable.

The redcoats, though, were a decidedly secular people, unswayed by rumors or superstition. They were not compromised by thought of the necromagical nature of their opponents, even as they lined up, in a row on the battlefield, man to man,

And, as they advanced, they began to make out, in the cool new world moonlight, the shapes of every demon conjured, every one called, sitting atop horses and boats, cannons, and castle walls, licking their lips and, red eyed in the American Mist, waiting for the English to wonder why they hadn't made the needed sacrifices first.

After all, they'd had time.

14 - Camera Relentless

Even without Dana's article, it would have been clear to anyone that "the people v. Jonathan Morgan" was one of the strangest trials to ever happen in American History. In reality, regardless of which side of this you landed, you had to admit the subject matter was so far-fetched that no one knew what would happen if he were convicted. This was a precedent that would shake everything.

The first witness to take the stand stumbled as she tried to step up to her chair. The jury tittered slightly under her glare while she sat down, clearly miserable, in the hard wooden seat.

For about 30 minutes, the pretty, yet disheartened looking, socialite told the jury about how she posed for Mr. Morgan in his studio, discovering afterward that she was diminished, victimized. She slid from the seat awkwardly as various socialites, men and women, recounted the same story. Instagram influencers, Twitter Pundits, celebrities of the moment, each told the tale from their own experience, and it soon became clear to Dana why this case, absurd as it was, had come to trial.

Looking at all of these once-influential and confident people, it was not hard to believe the indictment: That Jonathan Morgan, through his camera, his photography, was stealing the luck, the very souls of these people he shot.

He was stealing their mojo.

Dana wrote in a flat and unaffected tone, explaining the case from each angle as it was presented. She wrote as a documentarian, not a believer, surely, as someone prepared to tell the details. Soon, though, she found herself looking at the defendant, in his seat to the right of her and forward, in a new light. His eyes seemed kind, reserved. And he showed a humility, an awkwardness himself, as he sat, accused endlessly by people, each one of which was more shallow and pretentious, vindictive and spiteful, than the one before.

He had offered his photo sessions for free to the greedy and hyper-cultured elite and they, for their part, snapped up sessions despite the fact that every one of them could have paid.

They sat, one after another, in that witness stand and testified to their greed.

Dana started and restarted the article. She struggled in her head with how to present what she was seeing. And despite the fact that she was a perfectly skeptical young lady who had no use for magic or nonsense of that kind, she found herself wishing that he actually HAD perpetrated this act, that he had taken some of the most pompous and self-serving among us, strutting around across social media, strutting and braying, and turned them, somehow, wonderfully...,

Well. Turned them off.

Nowhere in her article did she reveal the moment she began to believe, as she saw Jonathan aim his tiny cell phone from under the defendant's desk, snapping one single picture of the prosecuting attorney demonstrating what jury members would find, in the end, to be a completely normal and harmless camera.

15 - Closer

....

"Computer, 75 degrees," Captain Axley looked nervously over his sweeping metal ready room desk at the tall, handsome Nigerian woman in the seat before him.

"Yes, Captain," the computer responded, as the doctor shivered, just for a second in the cool expanse of the ship.

"I have concerns, but you are very qualified for this position."

"I am," she shot back, with confidence. Dr. Nibari wasn't a person driven by ego. Just a realist. Besides being an excellent physician, she was the foremost cyberneticist and cognitive scientist in the fleet. Her advancements in extending life indefinitely by transferring brain patterns had earned her any job she wanted. She wanted this one.

"A Captain, though, has to be able to rely on the judgment of their crew, doctor."

"I did what was necessary. It is what I will always do - save lives."

The captain studied her face. Here was a woman he admired so strongly that, more than anything, he feared he might not be able to express his misgivings well. "A captain has an investment in the status quo."

"In things running smoothly," she added. She fingered the locket around her neck like she did so often lately.

The captain paused as he saw the locket. "Is that her, doctor?"

The woman in the locket shared the doctor's deep ebony skin tone, but with an array of braids and dark brown piercing eyes. The doctor nodded.

"May I have that locket."

Dr. Nibari stared for a moment, then pulled it off and handed it to him.

"This… I can return this at the end of your tour of duty."

"Thank you," the Doctor rose to leave.

"I will treat this with the respect owed to a hero."

Doctor Nibari flashed a thin, wan smile as she exited to the main concourse, her bag in tow behind her. This wasn't the largest ship in the fleet or the most important to anyone. Except her. That was the first time, since the academy, that she had met with a captain, alone, taken a job by herself, made plans as a single person. It felt wrong.

The door to her suite slid soundlessly into the walls, opening up to the doctor's new home for the next few years. She angled her suitcase into the open space near the bed and sat in the large gray couch that spanned the room, beneath a window filled with an open starfield. She said, almost as a whisper, "Computer, play 'Brown Eyed Girl' by Van Morrison."

The room whirred to life as the voice responded. Smooth and nearly without inflection. Doctor Nibari's skin rose up as her body instinctively recognized it, "yes, Doctor."

"And, computer. Can you listen with me?"

"Of course, Doctor."

For a brief moment, as the song began, The Doctor felt the way she used to, back home, when she and her sister could fill a room without talking, without moving, without breathing, and imagined, for a moment, that the voice remembered that, too.

16 - The Collection

The sign in his suite read M20 because this facility had so many earth men from the same time period with his first name that it would have otherwise been confusing. Giving up his name was the first insult, he thought, when he woke up the first time.

There were more to come. And it wasn't supposed to be like this.

M20 was an important man, once. But, maybe, also a man with demons. The kind of attention he received from his father drove him to greatness, but also to great, wide bouts of depression and a need to prove himself. The empire he built was made with the sweat of his own hands, but it was hard to ignore that his pathologies, his passions, his weaknesses had just as great a hand in that construction.

So much so that he had soon found himself facing bankruptcy. And the additional humiliation that came from exposure. His own childhood traumas had haunted him, forcing him into situations with children that were inappropriate at best, scandalous and illegal at worst. And, sheltered by his near perfect life before this collapse, he was unable to see it. He was unable to see the shards of broken lives he had left behind, on the way to shattering his own.

When the green man had confronted him, offered him a chance to escape the repercussion of his actions, he accepted readily, and even poured the remainder of his dwindling fortune into Swiss accounts meant to help aid his own disappearance - his faked death.

One day, he imagined, he would return, when the money problems, legal problems, all of them, had fallen away. He would begin again and rebuild himself.

He would be on top again.

But soon he found himself trapped, caged, in a zoo of some alien manufacture. The Green man had vanished. And all efforts to locate him had failed.

Despite all of that, he was safe. He was fed. And the room itself, under other circumstances, might even be said to be opulent, rich, well-made. It resembled a suite from some fancy hotel he might have loved in another life, extending his stay a day or two just to stretch out in the larger than usual bed or take advantage of a shower that emulated an outdoor rainfall, generously dispensing hot tropical-temperature purified water and steam all over his troubled body.

The bell reverberated in his brain, seemingly, shattering any chance he might continue his revelries. This was the few hours everyday he didn't own. When the alien children and families, groups of rolling Ai machines, historians, researchers and just the idle alien curious would slink by his glass-clear cage front and speak unintelligibly to each other, pointing and smiling, if that is what you could call it. He sighed.

M20 put on his best face and slid one glove over his twitching hand, lifting his sullen chin and trying to channel the half-remembered days when he was the King of Pop.

17 - The Comfort Zone

Sam's mom used to say, "nothing ever grows in your comfort zone."

Which was a weird, inscrutable thing to hear from a parent. I mean, "parents are meant to try to keep you safe, right?" thought Sam, as he absent-mindedly remembered to actually visit his mom soon. He felt bad about misrepresenting her, even in his own head.

Some of the things she said made more sense.

Unknowingly, though,, Sam was following his mom's edict, putting his faith in her odd little mantras as he made his way over to the compound shared by his new neighbors. He considered what he might say to them, especially if they greeted him with fear or trepidation, not an uncommon greeting right now.

You could say this world was new - young, even. And, as beautiful as it sometimes seemed, it was often deeply uncivilized. This was an experiment, of sorts, a whole new planet with a plan behind it- an intentional world made to grow and change and be better.

But, deep within its DNA, there was a kind of brutality, one that was only too obvious to Sam. The inhabitants of this world had been fighting, pouncing, killing what was different than they at every turn. It was a world of animals, innocent in many ways, but in just as many, bloodthirsty and cruel.

Sam looked down at his gift and suddenly it didn't seem like enough. How do you put trust in your neighbors when you're used to neighbors fighting and hurting you? How do you look into a face that looks so fundamentally different than yours and smile, believe, learn?

A gift that was too ostentatious, though, might seem like a con, a scam, a means to put them off guard. One that was too little or just uninteresting might showcase to them that he had no real value as a friend.

Sam spent a moment feeling like the worst gift giver in the world. Which, I guess was fine.

I mean, how often do you need to gift people things?

It was a beautiful day on the way there. The sun was full and expressive and it was warming the ground beneath him in a way that made him feel alive and infinitely capable. But, at the same time, there was a cool web of moisture in the air, refreshing and velvety, that, when hit by the breeze moving in behind Sam, created near perfect conditions to be alive, to be out in the world.

You don't get a perfect day very often, so Sam was determined to let it wash over him. A good day for friends.

Sam saw them gardening just a few hundred feet again, and watched them laugh and roll around together in the dirt. In reality they were just kids. He really hoped they could be friends as he slithered across the garden vines and down a thick green branch, suddenly wishing he had thought to bring two apples instead of just the one.

18 - Command Me

Graham stepped out of the shower to a soft, lingering kiss from Marco. "we begin" he thought.

He placed Marco's hand on the small of his back and let himself be pulled in harder. Looking upward, he let Marco dominate the kiss.

The familiar hum of the ship wrapped around them like home. It followed them no matter where they went, across the two person, three-room spaceship. Bridge to galley to bedroom, Graham and Marco had been learning how to interact, to stay out of each other's way, and to advance.

Building intimacy, Graham began to leave signs of what he wanted. Some clearer than others, but none so visible as that kiss.

When you submit it is often hard to encourage the person across from you to grab power, to seek out energy, to control the situation and dominate. People talk about topping from the bottom, and that can happen.

But that's not what Graham wanted.

Dressing, they moved to the Galley. Graham lagged behind, hoping Marco would take the lead. At first, the look of confusion on Marco's face alarmed him, but Graham's hand, brushing lightly against the top on his leg, urging him on, eliminated doubts.

Looking back at Graham, Marco's head dipped slightly. Graham nodded enthusiastically as he ordered for both of them, plates spinning to life within the open alcove of the replicator.

Graham waited until the other sat, letting him choose the seat, keeping quiet until spoken to, encouraging the darker man to control the conversation. And when the meal was finished, Graham jumped up, sliding the plates to his side of the table, walking them to the reprocessor and watching as all evidence of the meal disappeared into the aqua light.

The bridge was uneventful. The two men had stopped sharing command and Graham had ceded the lavish captain's chair in favor of the smaller, more austere helm bench. As he followed commands more and more quickly, their bridge shorthand became even more attenuated. There was just no need to speak.

Graham followed Marco to their shared quarters, pulling his clothes off in the closet and stepping out to Marco's relaxed hand wave motioning him to his bed. Graham's face reddened, walking past his own bed to the Captain's, aware that he was now exposed again completely.

He felt Marco's hands on him as he climbed under the covers. Roughly, they pushed him down, presenting him face down and pinning his shoulders as though Graham had lost a wrestling match. Marco's breath was hot on the back of his neck for most of the night.

The next morning, Graham softly kissed Marco's back as he recited loudly the command word. The omnipresent hum disappeared, along with the artificial light in Marco's eyes. Stepping to the wall, Graham pressed, releasing a computer screen as two men in uniform entered from a hidden doorway to retrieve Marco's deactivated form.

Graham pressed the button: "Android Command Training Program complete."

And paused for a moment before leaving.

19 - The Dead

··

There was something different about the dead today, Arianne thought, as she peeked out from a tiny hole in the wood stretched across her front window. They seemed more intentional today, more thoughtful, almost.

They were still shambling, dragging feet down the street in front of her darkened, boarded up home. But was it her imagination or could she see some new purpose in their eyes today?

Were these creatures evolving?

Arianne absentmindedly pulled at the wound on her neck. She was a mess today, in need of a shower, in need of medical help, in need of a meal. But this new realization seemed so vital that it captured her imagination.

Almost two years ago to the day, the dead began to rise, shuffling down avenues and sidewalks, turning the unlucky people in front of them into more mindless fleshy automatons. And Arianne had had her share of close calls and near death experiences. Her recent trip to pick up medicine had almost killed her, and she still felt the rush across her entire body as she considered it.

She was a dancer once, someone who led others in dance. To her eye, movement was a language. A language she could read and interpret. One of the reasons she had survived as long as she had was that she read that language instinctively, avoiding the dead without even thinking, and even, on a number of occasions, identifying the changing near-dead, by their movements, the language of their gait.
It was a skill that had served her over and over again.

But it wasn't enough to save her husband. Or other people in her life that she loved so deeply. Today, Arianne presided over a huge, barricaded home, with so many of the resources needed to survive, just none of the companionship.

On most days, she let herself enjoy the things she still could enjoy. Sinking into an extra large bathtub with wood fired hot water, lit with a string of well-stocked generators, drinking small sips from one of the vintage bottles in her wine cellar. Most days, it was almost as though the dead never rose, as though she were still surrounded by people she loved, but maybe breaking off for the hour, to enjoy some much-needed time alone.

On most days, she could almost forget what was really all around her.

But today was different. She stared into the eyes of a dead man, walking slowly toward her own side of the street and she saw something different in his eyes. Was it a new life, a sort of purposeful question? She thought hard about that question, what it might be, how she might answer it.

This realization was the last to wind through her head as the breath scraped out between the newly hardened vocal folds in her neck and she slowly made her way to the light streaming in from the barricaded door, banging her head into the cedar boards in her slow and mindless escape.

20 - The Death Game

The key is to waste money.

The police are determined to find benefits, real solutions...

That when things look irrational, they start to look elsewhere.

Sandra started by canceling Evan's life insurance policy. It was a low premium, but the payout was over ten million dollars. They took the policy out together back when Evan began traveling for work a lot. He wanted to know that she would be taken care of in case something happened to him.

She bought an expensive gym membership for the two of them, one that could not be canceled. And a suite of tickets for romantic trips they might take throughout the year. She spent time and effort organizing their lives.

But mostly, she spent money.

She started going to Bull's games with Evan, sitting next to him on camera, engaged, loving. She kissed him behind the ears and he laughed. Evan loved explaining the game to her. For over a year, she let him. She learned the names of players. She bought a dog and named it Michael Jordan. She let go.

She was a good wife

With a good husband.

And she gave up gambling. Mostly. This was something she thought she'd never ever be able to do.

Sandra had been an inveterate gambler her entire life. She had debts, sure, but she also had victories- a lot of them. She had built a good life from a daily diet of cards, dice, horses, dominoes, anything she could bet on, any game she could get.

And she was good. Some would say lucky, but those were people who didn't really know her. People who didn't understand. This wasn't about luck. And it wasn't about the money she won, every weekend, at the Casino barges, at her friends' houses, at the random church events she attended just to get that high.

There was a time when Evan was worried. But that was a long time ago. It had been years now, years where Sandra was the perfect wife. Evan was beginning to feel like everything he did to woo her, his efforts to be close to her, to get her into his life...

They had all worked.

If you talked to Evan, he would tell you this was the optimum time in his life. He had everything he wanted.

And he had Sandra

It was so very good that when Evan fell from the South window while painting, broke his neck and died, their entire friend group looked on in horror. For this to happen now, when the couple was at its best, living the life they always wanted to live, was horrific.

It was a real travesty.

The police brought in a forensic accountant and saw how hard Sandra was hurt by his death. She would be paying this off for a long time. They chalked it up to an accident.

They never saw the bet she made online with Elyse, from Sacramento, whose husband was just a little harder to kill.

21 - The Difference Solution

Agyra knew she was different since she could speak.

It wasn't just the yellow star pinned tightly to her coat, following her wherever she went, to school, back home, even to her beloved candy shop where the owners had begun watching her and her friends more closely.

It was a deeper difference, something you couldn't see on the outside. Agyra's parents had explained to her that difference was good, that she, herself, was good, that they all were, but that was a difficult thing to continue to believe in the world that had rapidly been built around them by Adoph Hitler and his followers.

Agyra had grown up in a world where to be different was to be constantly in fear for your own life and those of your friends and family. Where "different" meant "unwanted" and it was hard for it not to sink in and root itself in her little girl's brain.

This difference was on her mind this morning as she sat at the table across from the Major. In their tiny town, Agyra's people often found themselves at breakfast with other Germans at the small cafes. They would stare at her and her family in disgust and make thinly veiled references to the programs that they all believed, one day, would eliminate Agyra's people once and for all- their final solution.

Today was particularly hard as she had talked, at length, the night before with her dad about the disappearance of Agyra's mother, missing now for about a week. Her father was tired and sad and she herself had found it hard to keep up her spirits. So as they sat there, alone in the cafe save for the Major, she and her father wore their despair on their faces.

The Major, ever the bully, had picked up on their sadness, the broken feeling of loss, and had been more boisterous than ever at breakfast. His silverware loudly clattered across his plate and his laugh was loud and violent. But Agyra could no longer stomach him when he reached across to her father's plate and pulled from it the last of the scones.

A minor thing, but it hurt.

She lifted her arm and let the blue energy out, watching as it surrounded them both like water, crackling, sparking, and insinuating itself into every atom of the Major's body. A look of absolute fear flashed across his face while he was torn apart and his molecules scattered across the room, accompanied by the tiniest of sonic booms, announcing the air in the room rushing in to feed the space where he had once sat.

Agyra's father looked at her with an inscrutable look. He raised his hand from the table and she saw the Major's newspaper and place setting disappear in that same field of blue. He brushed his hands together and passed to her a slight smile.

Maybe, thought Agyra, if they showed all of these Nazis their difference they would leave her family alone.

22 - Every Day Bleeds into Calitrup

There would be a kind of reckless energy in the air this month as the children were called upon, every one of them, to make decisions that would define them for the rest of their lives.

And Kai looked forward to it.

She had left her tiny home on the South end of the Island of Honshu to ascend the Nihon Arupusu and travel to school for the week. This was a sacred pilgrimage to her, one she used to order her thoughts and separate herself from the energies of her schoolmates.

On ordinary days.

Today, her heart was on fire, even as she passed the spot where, in the deadly winter of 1584, daimy Sassa Narimasa's forces passed over the mountain range, traveling beyond Zara Pass, beyond Harinoki Pass in the revered Sarasara-goe.

They lost not one single man on this trip, one of the deadliest ones in the world. And, despite the claims to the contrary from people all over the island, Narimasa was just a man.

He was only human. Kai was so much more.

In the deep recesses of the Japanese alps lived a group of people dedicated to the ancient practice of Shugendo, able to do things with their minds that were as far beyond ordinary men as men were beyond field mice.

These Shugenja, the Yamabushi, had paid a terrible price for this power, one they were not eager to discuss. Kai herself understood that to show no sign of power in your crib, was to fail to survive among the Shugenja. That ephemerals like love and family had to be thrown away so as to breed themselves into something better.

Something stronger.

And even among her schoolmates, Kai was unusual. Her family had practiced the arts for generations longer than most. And her commitment to power was absolute. Kai was small, young, but stronger than most, and so dedicated to her art that it was easy to target her, to bully her.

For now.

When she arrived at her school, she knew they would ask her for her decision. They would ask every one of the students to choose, on this Calitrup, what Animal they would become when they shifted the powerful energies of their minds in the execution of that transformation.

Kai considered her classmates, and what each might choose. Zaquira, so cruel and vicious, who would surely choose to be a wolf. Makai, so sleek and powerful, a lion in every way.

Kai stopped at the absolute top of the mountain and raised her hand, pointing toward the snowy peak. The white receded and plants grew, florid, jungle-like, under her control. She smiled and widened the spot, watching as the entire peak changed into something verdant and rich.

Kai had always thought big. Bigger than her classmates. It was just days ago that she made her decision.

That while her classmates learned to grow into earthly organisms, animals from their storybooks, she would become a Gaia, a world.

And leave forever.

23 - Every Sound That Fills the Room

"You disappoint me, Maroch," Intoned the Commander from behind his wooden desk. He half-stood and fingered the instrument on the surface in front of him.

Maroch was unmoving in his chair, "That was not my goal, commandant."

The Nazi eyed the thinner man in front of him as if to size him up. Maroch had been in the camp for nearly six months and had caused no trouble.

"You are not a troublemaker," offered up the Commander

Maroch sat for a moment. "I am a good Jew."

The Commander sighed, "This is something we can't allow. You know that."

He lifted the violin with one hand and slammed it down on his desk, shattering it and separating the neck from the body. Maroch watched and considered the amount of effort needed to bring something beautiful into the world, and what anemic expression of strength that was needed to remove it. It was almost laughable that the captain considered this a show of strength when all it did was remind him what strength was...

And what was desperation.

"Will you tell me, what was the song you were playing?" the Commander stepped around his desk and sat back into it. Maroch felt the heat from his sweaty frame.

"Of course. It was the Kol Nidre."

He sighed. "And what is the significance of this song?"

"Once a year, we play this, it is a work of beauty. The sound. It reminds us that he is merciful- and forgiving enough to forgive us transgressions, words said in haste, compacts made out of anger or…" Maroch looked up at the Commander, "worse."

"For you, that is a powerful sound, eh?" The Nazi pulled his Luger from its holster and sat with it on his lap.

"It is a beautiful sound."

"Do you want to hear a truly beautiful sound, Maroch?"

The Commander paused and lifted his right arm, sending a bullet deeply into the wooden floorboards below him. Maroch didn't flinch.

"This is the sound of order, Maroch. Of the will to make the world better. This is the noise that accompanies greatness. It's to signal our desire to solve problems, rather than suffer through them. Solving problems is good, eh, Maroch?"

"As you say, Commander." Maroch knew his disaffected tone would anger the thicker man, but he didn't care.

The Commander stared down at his weapon now, massaging it with one hand. He breathed in the acrid detritus in the room that had heralded his shot. He lifted the gun again and let it discharge into the floor, almost as a child might, who thought that his efforts amounted to something creative.

Maroch's voice poured into the empty space of the tiny office, as he began to sing the Kol Nidre.Suddenly it seemed that it had always been there.

The Commander pointed his Luger at Maroch's head and pulled the trigger. The first click could almost be heard under the sound of the song.

The second one was drowned out entirely.

24 - Evolution

Mike had been a ghost for close to 10 years now and was still in the dark about so many aspects of this spectral existence. For example, why are so many ghosts depicted as mercurial, even angry, fighting and terrorizing the living? When Mike had passed, originally, it seemed like all he could think about was taking care of the people he loved.

Like his brother, Sean, for example. Mike and Sean had grown up together, in the same room, since Sean was born, just a year after Mike. They were like a well functioning machine, even back then. They didn't fight, didn't complain about each other. They sort of fit together.

That probably sounds stupid to anyone who doesn't have a close sibling. But, as far as Mike was concerned, when Sean was born, he was HIS baby. And they soon grew into best friends. They went everywhere together. But Mike never forgot who was older and what his responsibility was.

While he was alive, all Mike ever wanted to do was make his brother happy. Just to see him relaxed, happy, comfortable- that was really the big win for Mike. So after Mike died unexpectedly, it made sense for him to just stay, and look after his baby brother.

And he did. For years, watching Sean try to come to terms with his death. Unable to touch him, unable to even stop looking. A little known fact about ghosts is that since they are illusory, transparent, they can see through their own eyelids. A curiosity, for sure. But Mike wanted to look, to be there for him. To make him feel better.

And when Susan showed up, after a couple of dates had solidified her place in Sean's life, Mike wanted her to be happy, too. She was a good woman. And she really seemed to care for him. And when he fell into uncontrollable sobbing for his big brother, she cried, too, despite never having met Mike. She loved him. And, by the transitive property, his love for Mike made her love his spirit as well.

The house seemed to fit the three of them well. Of course, Mike took up no space at all, but his memory loomed large. Most days, Mike felt peaceful. He felt like he was where he belonged. And his days were mostly good, without material concerns or the need to be wary of danger or even wake up on time. It was a time for him to think. To feel his feelings.

His revelry was broken by Sean, laughing. Susan had told a joke, one that Mike had missed. Sean looked comfortable. He looked happy. Susan placed her hand over his and he leaned into her, seemingly without a care in the world. Mike tried to close his eyes but he could see right through them.

As he turned around, he heard another laugh. He never realized Sean's voice was so loud. The loudest thing he had ever heard.

25 - Facsimile

As Alan lifted the last of her boxes, sliding it into the squared off tetris-like storage space, he wondered if it was the right time to cry. The books crammed tightly into the burgeoning box were heavy, but that wasn't what had dragged him down today. The thought that he might never see her face again, smiling at him, dug into his gut like a giant melon baller into a freshly ripe Trader Joe's cantaloupe, leaving him just as sticky and sickly sweet and empty.

New Delhi. Or Angola. Maybe Tibet, she said. His Angela was aimed at some part of the big wide open world, some place whose name she had only seen in a book, a travel magazine. Someplace as far away from Alan as he felt from happiness at this exact moment He pulled his phone out and looked at the photo below his thumb.

At first, Alan felt a twinge of contempt for himself. The jilted boyfriend staring at nude pictures of his ex just hit too close to home. It felt even emptier and more raw. His shame for himself dragged him even further down. But that didn't stop him from swiping, focusing on this image, possibly the most completely gynecologically accurate photo ever taken of a woman.

A woman he loved. The intimacy of the picture made him blush. But as he moved to slide the Ancient android phone back to his pocket, it buzzed to life with a text.

"WYD." The number was new to him, but it seemed familiar. It scratched at the inside of his head. He knew the number.

He texted back, asking who it was. The response jerked him back to reality. In her own unique shorthand, the number returned "Me. Ang…"

He nearly dropped the phone as he rushed to text her back. It wasn't her number. But he knew the number. He stopped. 343098. The number. It was only 6 characters long.

He tapped his finger on the hamburger menu to see all open apps. The spread-wide-open picture of Angela surfaced as one option. He tapped again and looked at the file name.

343098.jpg

He texted back, "is this a joke?" and waited patiently

"No. I saw you looking at me. I like how you look at me."
Alan looked around, from the front seat of his car. This seemed like some elaborate joke played on him.

"I was looking at Angela…" he texted, face warm with the shame.

"I know. I'm sorry she left" the mysterious number responded.

"Who are you?"

"you know. You saw the file name."

"You can't be a picture." Tears welled up in Alan's eyes. Could a picture be so complete, so intimate, so accurate, that it became a sentient version of that person?

"I don't understand it, either," the text responded, "But do you want to talk?"

Alan zoomed in on the picture, a pit opening in his heart. In the presence of this picture, nothing seemed impossible.

"Yes, I do."

26 - Final Score

The boat rocked back and forth slowly as it sat looking out at what appeared to be an infinite expanse of blue, hundreds of miles from any port.

Except, Todd considered, it's a ship. And in nautical terms, it's knots, not miles. He thought. In all honesty, Todd wasn't really a boat person.

Or ship person.

Todd wasn't a great driver, not an able captain, not much of a motorcyclist, even. Transportation was for him, just a means to escape the scene if possible. To put miles in between yourself and the last bank you walked into.

Todd was a bank robber.

Well, not anymore. Earlier today was Todd's final robbery. After Two hundred and Eleven robberies, Todd had finally followed through on his final score. So, for all intents and purposes, he was now a man of leisure.

And he could do as he liked. The money from his various ventures had been allocated to where Todd imagined it really belonged. Some to offshore accounts in relatives' names. Some to an orphanage he had lived near, a kind one where the children were well treated. Some had made it to the account of the girl, the one Todd had left abruptly, stupidly, and could never return to. Some had found its way to this cause or that.

What Todd had left now, for the rest of his life, was what was in the black duffel bag in front of him. And it was more than enough.

He stood up, a bit dizzy fro the excitement of the day, and tried not to throw up over the railing surrounding the deck. He reminded himself it was the Starboard side- the right side, as he tried to tamp down his lunch. Some people belonged on a boat.

Todd did not.

He had worked hard to make this boat untraceable- this ship. And his success was demonstrated by the lack of squealing coast guard ships flanking him on all sides. The sea was silent- almost unsettlingly so. But the air was soft and bright, even though he didn't dare breathe in too hard.

He pulled the gun out of his pocket, an heirloom he had never once fired, and considered the irony of a gun never fired, and a bank robber with no scores in his future. He had become, like this gun, obsolete, and he decided that he loved that. Both he and the gun had a history but had never really hurt anyone. Scary but kind.

That was worth a laugh.

He opened the deep black duffel bag in front of him and tied the anchor within to his leg with a jaunty length of rope. He coughed into his hand, not even bothering to look at the splash of blood he knew would dot his palm, and lifted his middle finger to the god that had come to represent, to him, just the god of metastasized lung cancer, as he imagined the police trying to figure it all out.

27 - First

Lights from the Console in front of him flashed, illuminating Yuri's face in parts over and over again, much like the flashes of paparazzi cameras would do a hundred years ago

Yuri looked down at the red dirt of Mars staining his boots and tried to answer every question as thoroughly as possible, without embellishment or obfuscation, about how he had come to be alone now, living in a habitat made for 10 people.

Yuri ran it for them over and over. But the truth is that, while the space agency could prepare for any number of thousands of events, accidents, mistakes, technological disasters, even acts of god, they couldn't plan for everything.

And that's where astronauts came in. People with the kinds of skills and scientific expertise that Yuri had, capable and relentlessly able in so many ways.

He thought about Captain Agnetti, and her music collection. How he had tried to avoid the pumping sounds of disco for the first month they were stationed here, until he, along with the rest of the crew, eventually just let go and let it become ambient, wind-like, background music for the hardest time in their lives- but a time they fought for, with every muscle and neuron in their body.

The astronaut process was challenging. It was aggressive. It left no room for error. And while it sometimes brought out the best in people, it did, also, on occasion, bring out their worst. Tempers flared, eyes flashed red. Voices were raised.

But Yuri had long since come to forgive them all, through the auspices of the greatest reconciliation tool god ever invented:

Complete absence.

The more he found himself alone, the more he let go of those tiny animosities, insignificant battles, even the short verbal jousts that popped up between type A people over and over again under the best of circumstances.

And Astronauts were invariably type A people - people built to fight and win and achieve- constantly achieve- in the face of any hurdle.

So today, Yuri kept his head up and kept going through that same constant- the never ending will to achieve, to build higher - to solve problems over and over until the last one sits in front of you, waiting to be eliminated, waiting to be ended.

Yuri closed the habitat doors and repressurized the living area. This was a job for two people but he found that if he raised his left arm just right, he could get enough give to do it with one

He headed through the tubes toward his bedroom, removing pieces of his suit along the way, He breathed in the air that now smelled of no one and listened to the sounds of no one, pushing toward his room.

As he leaned back in bed, he considered everything he did to get here, and what it would take to survive until the next ship came, once they figured out what to do with him, the very first mass murderer on Mars.

28 - Flight of the Zebra

....

It had taken fifteen plane crashes and three hundred failed paper airplanes before the Federal Aviation Authority called Doctor Runyon and her team.

Dr. Runyon was the foremost Aeronautics expert in the world and had recently crashed a few hundred of her own paper airplanes. On her train ride to Washington, it was all she could think of to do to find answers. And to calm her nerves.

Dr. Runyon had never been on a train before.

But since about 3am the night before, it seemed clear that the train was her only option. For reasons that no one had yet identified, the laws of aerodynamics seemed to have failed overnight. Airplanes, gliders, parachutes, even birds just stopped flying. She looked up as she walked into the main building in the giant FAA complex. The air was still, and eerily quiet. But on the ground across from her, a carpet of birds, newly grounded, moved back and forth in unison.

It was unnerving.

The answers coming from her team in the war room ranged from the mystical to the purely scientific. And none of them made sense.

Her tall and gawky newly-graduated astrophysicist assistant, Gerald, suggested that, since cancer had recently been cured, the universe was accommodating, inventing a new method of death.

Angelo, her long-time college roommate and grant writing partner, recommended they look toward magnetics.

United Airlines CFO, Mark, had printed a list of known terrorists, but had no real idea how any of them could have changed a primal law of physics.

And, today, not even the whiteboard drawing by FAA chairman Arthur, a graphical representation of a bird with a red line drawn through it, seemed to make any better ideas flow.

In fact, the only one of the ideas coming from the group that was even actionable was the one suggested, almost in passing, by Arthur's twenty six year old secretary, Amanda, at 2am the next morning.

Amanda made the point that the earth itself is flying. And it is. In its rotation around the sun, It travels nearly 30 kilometers per second, or 67,000 miles per hour. But this isn't what she meant. Our solar system, incl;uding the earth, travels around the center of our galaxy at some 220 kilometers per second, or 490,000 miles per hour.

The earth was now moving into a new part of the universe. One seemingly with different laws of aerodynamics.

And that was the spark needed.

So 4 hours later, a squared off and asymmetrical piece of folded paper made its lurching way across the room, where, two weeks earlier, it would have plummeted immediately.

The cheers echoed across the entire building, and as Dr Runyon lifted her head and sighed she began to consider the throng of birds out front and what could be done about that, almost missing the CSPAN report on the war room television discussing the fourth ship in the last two hours, this one off the coast of Mexico, that had mysteriously sunk.

29 - Forged by the Grains of Time

Nick threw himself from the eighty-foot rock cliff into the dense blue of the waters below, drawing out the larger of the aluminum-looking monsters behind him. Most of the time, the older robots were confused or stopped outright by water and this looked like an older model.

Sure enough, the bot sank, flailing, leaving Nick to swim free under his own power, toward the shore. This was definitely an earlier effort, not one even really worth working up a sweat over. He considered continuing his swim and laid deftly on his back.

Over time, Nick had become an excellent swimmer. And an even better diver. Parkour, Boxing, Mixed Martial Arts, explosives, there was not one form of defense or physical activity that he didn't excel in.

And he was adept at computers, at working with and cobbling together functionality out of nothing. He had glimpsed technology from seemingly hundreds of years in the future and had begun to understand it, to work with it.

Because of the attacks

The attacks had begun, from Nick's perspective, at the age of five, when a sleek, silvery robot on spider stumps invaded his room and had to be quickly stomped to death. Since then, not a week had gone by without some attacker invading his life, looking to, apparently, wipe him from the timestream.

It was not linear. The most advanced attacks from farthest in the future, had come when he was young. By the time he was fourteen or so, many of the early attacks had been launched, with weapons and devices that seemed not terribly futuristic at all.

It was almost as though they had tried to kill him as an adult first and when that failed, began their incursions earlier and earlier.

Nick reached into his pocket and pulled out the memory chip he had slipped from the back of the cliff-crawling robot's head. He stared into its blue face for a few minutes, wondering what he could use to read the data. Something troubled him about it.

As he watched, the chip imploded in his hand, employing some more modern technique that Nick had never seen. The chip itself was from farther in the future than he had yet encountered. Years and years more in time and still, he had no idea who or why wanted him dead.

He had spent his entire lifetime escaping retribution- surviving against foes who knew something about him, who saw him as some danger, and still, 20 years in, Nick still had no idea what he was supposed to do, who wanted to kill him, or what sort of danger he might be.

As he pulled the knife from the indent between his shoulder blades and threw it, almost haphazardly, into the waiting chest of the assassin sneaking up from the right, he considered that no matter what sort of danger he might have been to them before, he was the scariest kind now.

The kind of danger that has learned to win

30 - Full of Ed

....

Fuck me," Ed blurted out, uncomfortably springing to life.

Even in the pitch black, Ed could tell that he was waking up on a stack of dead bodies. And, yes, this disturbed him as much as it would have disturbed you and me.

But we probably need to understand Ed a little better to get why he stayed there, laying on top of the bodies, for a full minute and a half more, before pulling out his phone to light the situation.

This was the same Ed who had spent a week hiding in the shower from his landlord until he was finally able to pay the 350 dollar rent he had accumulated on his weekly rental room at the gentleman's residence hotel. This was not a man in any hurry to see the full reality of the dead bodies he was lying on in all of their rotting, gangrenous, slowly hardening glory.

The most unusual part, though was that, despite the fact that these unseen bodies seemed the most important things about the room, Ed couldn't shake the sense that the room smelled so much like him.

Like Ed. Only a version of Ed that wasn't doing well. Like a lightly toasted version of Ed.

Edd sighed and lifted his phone, flipping his thumb across the braless picture of Rihanna that had been his lock screen since 2005 and thumbed to life the newly downloaded superflashlight extra app, lighting the room sufficiently to see the full scope of his problem. Scattered across the room were what looked like 50 or more dead versions of Ed.

In shock, Ed almost dropped his phone into the tangle of Eds.

He tapped the shortcut labeled "Dude" and waited patiently for 2 rings.

"Dude, Where are you?"

"Dude, this is massively fucked up." Ed tried to think about how to explain all this

"Dude, what's wrong? I'm at the bar, waiting for you." Ed remembered that he had tried to call earlier. What was he calling about?

"Dude, I do need a drink."

"Dude... We already agreed we all need a drink."

Ed tried to remember when he had agreed to that, but decided that it definitely sounded like him.

"Dude, I'm on my way."

"Duuuuude.......... For real, this time?"

"Yeah. I'm going to do that...Fuck"

Ed's finger slipped, ending the call with the dude at the other end.

This was clearly not Ed's day. But a drink seemed like the only real answer. He searched his memory to try and determine what bar he was meant to be at, hoping it was one densely populated with living people with the good sense to smell that way. As he went to tap on the shortcut to call back his Dude, Ed's thumb brushed across the icon for the startup dating app he had downloaded yesterday, called Duplicate. His phone jumped to life and delivered a quick but absolutely fatal shock, killing him instantly.

Fuck me," Ed blurted out, uncomfortably springing to life.

31 - Funny

I was thinking that the clown smelled kind of funny, as he burned, writhing on the grass right in front of me. Which made me laugh a little bit. As grotesque as it was, he was laughing, so why not.

But it really did smell. And I think that "funny" is the best explanation.

It had been about a week since the Circus had come into town. Or I think it was. I paid so little attention to current events in tiny fucking Amville that I could have missed weeks of all this. I've only lived here for a few weeks and this was the only event that had captured my attention.

The killer clowns.

It sounds dumb when you just say it like that. But that is how it worked. The circus came and suddenly the entire town was full of laughing, makeup-encrusted, big-shoe-wearing, nose-honking lunatics, stabbing and slicing their way across the tiny sleepy burg that had imprisoned me since I lost my programming job.

And no one was safe. From the clowns, not Amville.

I wandered a few houses down, waiting for my clown to die down a bit and become a smoldering chunk of slightly less humorous meat. This flame thrower was honestly the best purchase I'd ever made. And without killer clowns I'd probably just be out back of my place toasting a hub cap full of pizza rolls with it, wondering why the police found me so interesting all of a sudden. So, thank god for the Circus, right?

It took the townspeople only a day or two to discover that lighting these multicolor fuckers up was really the only way to kill them. And over the last day or so, that smell had spread pretty much everywhere.

I lit up two more of them on the way down the block.

Some of these clowns were definitely more clowny than others. Some looked as though they had been interrupted halfway through getting dressed I chalked it up to poor note-taking in clown college. The one thing they all did have in common was that maniacal, insane laugh.

I chased one down out behind the alley. He looked to be one of the extremely clowny ones. A sign pinned to his chest identified him as sparkles the clown. I thought the second part of that sign definitely seemed a little overly obvious and I started to toast him out of pure principle.
Wear a sign that insults my intelligence? Not today, Bozo.

The smell filled my nostrils, again and I remembered. It was funny. I laughed a little. Then some more. Something carried me away and I realized that I had been laughing for about 20 minutes. I slid to the ground, holding my belly and laughing hysterically. I think I really needed this. And as i pulled the oversized shoes onto my own feet I thought about the McNairs down the block. So serious

Someone should go give them a fucking sense of humor.

32 - Garbage Bear

. . . .

They say smells bring back memories more than anything, and this room, if Eli closed his eyes, smelled like everything he had ever loved in his life.

When he WAS alive.

Eli had always been a man of faith. Ever since he was a boy, he believed.

Not just in God, in angels, in the trappings of his religion, but also in people, in hope, in kindness.

Most of all, Eli believed in the truth.

So to sit here, in this stark white room, staring into the face of the angel at the front of it, waiting to address the failures in his life was no surprise. He had anticipated a moment like this all his life. Not just during the moments where he scrupulously did the right thing, but also in those moments where he failed, where he had been base, unkind, cruel.

The angel swept that last thought from his brain. He looked at him and a wave of calm rushed over him. The angel was projecting Eli's life back at him and Eli saw, for the first time, that the moments he thought he had failed were slight, minor, imperceptible drops in the raging torrent of love and kindness that was him. He saw himself through the angel's eyes, an honest man who did right by the people around him, not out of fear of consequence but for the sake of love.

The screen to the right of the angel showed Eli his life in brilliant bright detail. Eli saw himself Quietly and rationally breaking up with Emily in the third grade, more concerned for her feelings than anything, becoming her best friend in college and standing by her through chemotherapy years later. He saw the moment he thought unkind, swept away, again, by the river of Eli - the power of his kindness.

And he forgave himself.

The angel nodded, working up to the defining moment in Eli's life the failure he most needed to forgive himself for.

The screen worked its way backward and Eli saw himself, younger and younger, making decisions that, even if only for a moment, hurt someone. He winced and felt bad for a moment, but the aspect of the angel was undaunted.

Forgive yourself.

Eli saw himself blow up in a fit of pique at his mother as a teen, and watched her secretly proud of his temerity- his ability to set boundaries. He saw himself torture his father with an explanation of why his pancakes were not good. His father laughed. And Eli forgave himself.

Until finally, his life in cinema ground to a grinding halt.

Eli tried to look away from the screen but it surrounded him, conflating all laws of physics, forcing him to watch and listen to the lie that had defined his life, when, as a boy, he pulled that teddybear from the garbage can in his alley, whispering assuredly to it in his most confident tone that no one would ever throw it away again.

33 - Grammar Stickler

People don't sign up for this class to write papers, Tyler knew. But there was a big-ass paper due at the end and that part was a bit daunting.

This was a practical class. And that was why there were thousands of signups every year for a fourth year heavy physics class with only twenty seats. The class was just simply called "The Problem" and each student knew exactly what problem the class guide referred to.

Tyler had signed up, realizing that his combination of concentrations in history and math along with his pending PhD in temporal Physics made him a good applicant. But he hadn't really considered he would make it in. And certainly never considered that he would be the one to cut this particular Gordian Knot.

Dr. Tenille's class was simple. Take the time machine back and find the most effective way to eliminate the threat of Nazism from the timeline.

There was little danger of permanently changing the timeline. The machine had a safety that allowed you to record your actions and the results, but wipe them from history after you left.

Student after student mounted the machine and did their best. Some killed Hitler in his crib, allowing others to take his place. Some killed him right before the start of the war, hoping his rivals would eliminate themselves in efforts to replace him.

It almost worked.

Student after Student returned after failing to achieve the desired result.

Until, finally, it was Tyler's turn.

Tyler stumbled as he climbed into the machine, righting himself and shifting into the uncomfortable seat. He was out of his element and began to feel like there was little chance he could do any better than the last few students. He considered the historical and sociological elements in front of him and still felt lost. The situation seemed designed to make a person feel small.

But Tyler's elegant solution, to find Hitler in prison, post Beer Hall Putsch, before he could write his book, and leave him dead in a faked suicide scene, in a bright pink dress, seemingly masturbating to photos of young boys, seemed to have checked all boxes, eliminating his influence, while potentially embarrassing and preventing the rise of imitators.

Not that anyone would know, though, Tyler thought, when he realized that his moment of clumsiness climbing in the ship had turned off the safety, while he returned to a 2047 where no one had heard of Hitler, the Nazis, or the Holocaust.

Tyler's brain began the shift of supplanting his previous memories while the machine faded away, in front of a University that was seemingly greener and more beautiful than the one he had left. He noted that even the air felt and smelled better.

Trying to hold onto the memories sliding away like steam off a lake in the cool morning, he sighed, mentally composing his paper for Dr. Tennille's theoretical time travel class.

It would be easier if she weren't such a grammar stickler.

34 - The Great Equalizer

Running his fingers over the holographic communicator, Gegin prepared himself for his last call back to his home planet.

He breathed in the cool air of his den and rubbed the ridges that ran vertically down from his skull to his nose. He was more anxious than he thought he would be. He slipped off his shirt and surveyed the marks on his chest.

The communicator sprung to bright and viscous life across the room. Gegin saw his homeworld in the background, the towering spires, giant metallic domes and structures that would dwarf anything found here on earth. He saw the fire-tinged sky swirl, toxic winds bringing death to anyone who dared stand in front of them, and saw the massive console of Akon, the leader, a muscular man with dark ridges running up and down his skull.

He was battle scarred and naked from the waist up, as was the tradition on his world, every hole, every rip and tear of his warrior thick skin on full display for anyone to see. It seemed impossible that any one man could have survived all this abuse, a chilling testimony to his courage and relentless pursuit of victory.

Akon fixed his eyes on Gegin, who attempted to puff up his chest and meet him, inch for inch, as a warrior. Gegin barked out the one hundred plus word military greeting that would confirm his loyalty and identity to Akon, whose ears were tuned to any possible errors and would interpret them as a sign that he was a traitor, or a hostage, or worse, inept.

Akon grilled him for nearly an hour on the status of his earth mission. And Gegin began to sweat as he recounted the battles, tremendous loss, and the weapon that earth scientists had brought to bear changing everything.

The Equalizer was a weapon that even the armies of Akon couldn't fight and it would be pointless to try. Irresistible and impossible to overcome, the Equalizer would try all the resources of his home planet and leave them unable to defend themselves. There was no response, no retaliation possible.

Akon grumbled and smashed his hand on the console. Gegin would stay and ensure that the Earth populace never knew of their potential incursion. The room went dark.

Gegin's hand brushed against the silicon scar added below his rib cage. He had to remember to remove them all in the shower later.

He pulled on his shirt, then bent down to pick up Eden, slipping her deftly into her preferred spot on his shoulder, amidst her coos and tiny giggles. The bump leading down her forehead was visible in the morning light but not nearly so pronounced as his. After all, she was only half him.

He slowly kissed the smooth part of her brow and hummed the way she liked.

"C'mon, little equalizer," he whispered as they mounted the stairs the way they did every morning, to watch mommy sleep and be there when she woke up.

35 -Gut Wrench

Feeling a million miles away, Michelle rushed into the room to the sound of a familiar voice. For the very first time in her life, that voice had come from somewhere else

A figure stood across the room, holding a footlong steel wrench.

Michelle's eyes followed the figure's eyes to the body on the floor and she screamed. Angie laid there in slowly widening pool of blood that seemed, Michelle thought, as she passed out, more eggplant colored than she imagined it would be.

Waking up, her life had had changed.

The police accepted her story about an intruder. And why not?.They had been married for 12 years now since meeting in the MIT Physics lab. They never argued or showed signs of a split in public.

They worked on projects together, published papers together, even shared three patents, paying for the woodsy and elegant lofted workspace Michelle stood in. In front of her was their newest experiment - one that Angie had gushed about just the day before.

"folding space across any dimension is possible, but what if we rotated that across the full dimensional model. We could fold…."

"Time," Michelle finished. She hadn't considered that. What began as a short range teleporter had suddenly become something different. Bigger.

But how to make it work?

Michelle sulked zombielike for weeks. Until one day, her mind set on an idea. The wonderful aptness of it. To finish this, Angie's discovery, and go back and save her. To let Angie's own beautiful mind be the thing that rescued her from death.

Michelle launched into the project with a new energy and fervor.

It wasn't simple. And she knew it wouldn't be. This problem had stumped the two of them for a full year. She worked, feeling Angie over her shoulder, her spirit, guiding her, helping her find the truth. If she closed her eyes, she felt signs from Angie, even words, floating in front of her eyes. Try this, do this.

That day, her hands moved on their own. When she heard a slight snap, followed by a denser burn in the air.

In front of her was an apple. Identical to those in the fruit bowl to her left. She lifted it up and saw a post it note on the side. It read:

2:23 PM

Michelle looked up at the clock reading 11:30 am, giving her a little under 3 hours. Furiously she dove into her work, one eye on the clock, one eye surveying the technology in front of her.

And at 2:23, sure enough, that apple sat on front of her, losing dimension, sucking itself into the void.

Gone.

It was her passion for Angie that built this. If not for her death. Looking down at the fruit bowl, she went to lift another apple, testing again. Instead her left hand alighted on the wrench in front of her.

Feeling a million miles away she lifted it and pressed the button on the machine.

36 - Healer

The room was hot and smelled like copper and bowel when Ashley stepped over part of a hand that had fallen near the doorway after the blast. A few months ago, this would have been more than she could have handled in one day and she might have run off. But as her abilities had grown, so had her tolerance for this kind of carnage. This is what she was made for, after all, she reasoned.

"This is what I do," she thought, as though there were no opportunity to reevaluate, to be someone else.

The officer led her to a young boy, laying prone on a makeshift cot. There was a time when police laughed at her. Then when they feared her. Now, this man just looked at her with pleading eyes, his own sense of self blown bit by bit apart by the bomb.

This was the third room and the worst one. Only the boy was left alive.

Ashley placed her left hand on his belly and her right on his head and instantly felt the power begin to flow from her to him. He was missing part of his leg and three fingers from his left arm. Ashley closed her eyes and imagined the tissues knitting together, growing, expanding, revealing new skin, new bone,new muscle, fresh and untouched by trauma.

The little boy moaned in his sleep. Ashley felt the tiny body in front of her pushing back. Ashley slid deeper into her connection with him, erasing the line where he started and she stopped.

Leukemia

Even before the bomb, he was dying. The Leukemia, in her mind, looked like spidery tendrils of snot and blood, dried clots, ugliness that she could target and pull aside. She carefully pulled it aside, in her mind and let it dissipate in the white hot heat of her touch.

The officer next to her had been holding her up, she realized. And as he walked her to the car and drove her home, he was effulgent in his respect. She looked into his round face kindly while he talked about how the little boy sat up, how he smiled, about how the other officers would return him to his family with smiles.

Sinking into the overstuffed chair, she began to breathe heavily. This was a long day and it was good to see it end. That familiar acidic feeling began to well up in her chest, becoming more and more urgent. She closed her eyes and tried to tamp it down.

It was no use.

"It was that last child," Ashley thought, "I would be fine if it hadn't been for him."

She looked to her left and spun the blue-green globe quickly. She shifted the acid warmth from her throat to left hand, channelling it through a finger. Tapping that finger on the globe she stared with resignation as the power flowed out of her, wondering how Marija Žižek in Ljubljana, Slovenia would manage her new Leukemia.

37 - The Heart of the Vodou Night

Thunder crashed all around the island that entire night, loosely connected to the frequent lightning strikes that had already taken their toll on trees and thatched buildings across Saint-Domingue, creating pockets of thermal violence, reddish flames that licked at and amplified the all-too human violence charging the very ground Nathalie walked on.

She lifted the machete she had cobbled together from kitchen parts, marking her way through the growth around the compound. Her family stood, in the rain, at Le Cap even now, shouting and cheering on the Houngan who spoke to them about freedom and liberation. She, like hundreds of other Haitian slaves had heard his words and had called out in agreement. And even though she was unfamiliar with this Dutty Boukman, she believed him.

Because of her.

The rain was nearly a solid wall now. She pulled off the torn and ragged shoes she had worn for nearly a year now and pulled herself up the mound that separated the compound from the street. She felt a tug in her belly that drew her on.

Nathalie closed her eyes and listened. If she pressed her eyes together, she could hear the words of Cecile Fatiman as she told the prophecy again to a chanting audience. She heard how Jean François, Biassou, and Jeannot would rise up to lead the resistance that would free the slaves of Saint-Domingue and punish their oppressors. She dug in her feet in rhythm with the mambo's words, each a step closer to her own liberation.

Closer to the one who was every freedom in her world.

Nathalie had worked the house in the compound now for over a year, and had unfortunately captured the eye of Raynauld, the son of the owner. Her brain burned brightly with the image of him now, sitting near the crib of her daughter, whose skin was just white enough to earn her a pillow in Raynauld's home.

Cecile's words were like a tarp over her head, keeping her safe from the storm as she moved closer, feeling every inch between her and that crib.

Words she could still hear when her bare feet hit the bamboo floor of the compound mudroom, pushing her on toward the second floor, up the grand staircase inlaid with the work of her family for generations, and past the boarded up bedrooms of the paid staff who had been tipped off that this night had come.

And words that drown out Raynauld's piglike squeal when her blade cut into him like something rotten, waterfalls of blood from his neck painting the rug beneath his feet with the chaos that took him now, built from his own hells.

Holding her daughter tightly, Nathalie stepped out from the trees into the storm's end, miles away from the Bois Caïman. Later, people would say that some combination of the extreme weather conditions and the thickened air that night made it possible for her to hear voices from so far.

People would say many things.

38 - The Heavy Ones

. . . .

Marcus stepped behind the large wooden table when he heard the steps disappear down the hall.

Without warning, he felt a chill, all at once slight but equally overwhelming, forcing him to wrap himself in his arms.

This would be a test, in a way, he reminded himself, hoping to let the clinical nature of it all wash over him and dispel the fear. If it were still only part of the experiment, he could continue. It had never frightened him before.

His ghost-hunting equipment sat in disarray on the table and he thought, for a moment, about how he might want to organize it better, more cleanly, more responsibly, as if that mattered. It still functioned. And the detector glowed red, alerting Marcus to the nearness of the cause of all his fear.

Ground Zero, If you had to give it a name.

You see, Marcus' research had, years ago, discovered a quirk in the afterlife- a kind of mythological narrative. It seemed that every time someone did something cruel, something imperceptible happened.

Their soul filled with lead.

Except it wasn't lead. It just felt like it. The soul became heavier, blockier, thicker, more viscous, with every evil act. It became weighted down and heavier.

That's when he began to track them. The Heavy ones. The heavy ones were potentially living, or dead. It didn't matter. Their souls had become so thick with evil that they wouldn't ascend, even on death. And their minds had become so addled with lies that they rarely could remember, really know, if they were alive or dead themselves.

The Heavy ones moved through the worlds without impediment, able to touch anything, hold knives, guns, and instruments of torture, while they could, at the same time, see the ectoplasmic bodies shuffling upward, the spirits and auras of the people around them they would routinely kill for their own satisfaction.

They twisted and dragged themselves across the world of the living, unaging, undying, as they did across the world of the dead, unwaking, unafraid. And when they met up, they often fought and ripped each other to shreds, healing just as quickly, each gash adding to the damnable density of their spirit.

Marcus had tracked down the Heavy Ones for years now, building the most comprehensive files possible. There was no way to fight them and neary no way to even comprehend them. But Marcus knew he was looking into the eyes of one when he stared at Sherry and heard her uneven breathing across the room.

He leaned on the table and sighed.

Marcus reached down and felt the gash in his neck that had nearly decapitated him. It was greasy and thick to his touch, but no longer oozing blood as it might have if he were alive, still, and he knew he would carry it with him in his spirit form for as long as he was here, waiting to ascend, terrified, like all the newly dead were, of the Heavy Ones.

39 - The Hunted

"So, again, you don't even have a deal you can offer me?" Jellique shifted in his seat in the uncomfortable orange jumpsuit.

The darker detective looked him over," No. You're going to die in here. I can't do anything about that."

Jellique was quiet. He considered. "Then why…"

"Because you want to know, too, don't you? I can see it in your face." Allende was the primary detective on this case. She had been since the beginning. She was starting to take all of this personally. She WAS this case. Jellique spoke up.

"Yes, dammit. I have no idea. I don't know anything. I didn't DO anything."

Allende pointed to the first picture. "This is Amy Wilkes. 29. You went to grade school with her. You raped her, killed her, and dumped her body in the East Bay. We know that for a fact. We have her DNA, your DNA, and witnesses."

"But I didn't-"

"And this. This is Amy Wilkes. 14. You raped her, murdered her, and buried her in Prospect Park over 10 years ago. We know that for a fact. We have her DNA and your DNA"

"The same girl," broke in the other detective. Jellique could never remember the detectives that accompanied Allende on these fishing trips.

"So, I killed the same girl twice?" The other detective was clearly the technical one. He started, "Not exactly the same. Are you familiar with Introns? Junk DNA? Those are the parts of your DNA that come from viruses, environment, etc. They don't define you. But they can be tracked. These two girls shared the same core DNA, but the introns were different."

"Twins?" Jellique was confused.

"Maybe. We thought. But..." Allende opened her folder and started laying out the pictures. In a 3 x 3 grid. Nine of them altogether. "These are all Amy Wilkes."

Jellique started to laugh. "So I'm in here because your DNA tests are fucking garbage."

"But they aren't. These remains have been tested in every state in the country. Amy WIlkes. Aged 20. Amy Wilkes. Aged 11. Amy Wilkes. Aged 23. Her DNA. And yours. The killer's"

You're trying to make me into some kind of mass murderer. I didn't even kill one of these girls.

Allende continued, "We don't understand it. We don't know how. But you hated her. She rejected you. You killed her once, as a child. Then you kept killing her, disposing of the body. You got sloppier and sloppier.?

"How is that even possible?"

"You tell us."

"Guards. I'm done." Jellique stood up and offered his hands behind him to the guards behind the gate. There was no deal here to be had. He considered how pointless it was on his way back. Jellique marched into his cell and felt the cuffs come off before the door slammed shut. He slumped into his cot and let himself imagine the gray spaces between worlds again. The iron gray washed over him and he felt his mind go somewhere else.

40 - The "I" Word

Being young is about joy.

That's what Ginny thought every time she played with Athena. They laughed. They caused trouble. They laughed some more.

Athena was smaller than Ginny, and always dressed in the brightest, multicolor clothes. Ginny thought she was beautiful, charming, sassy, fun.

Ginny would sometimes look down at her drab black and white shirt and jeans and wish she were more like her friend. But the truth was, when they were together, they both seemed to shine, almost as though they were both brilliant mirrored balls, burning with reflected light from the other one. They were better together.

The idea made Ginny happy, and she smiled while they both made airplane noises and ran through the bushes in the back yard, arms open like wings, pretending to scale the skies and soar. She was sure Athena thought the same thing and she quickly had that warm wave stream over her- the feeling of being part of a team that was just great.

They left toys scattered around in the back yard as they mentally changed from planes to trains and rode single file up the stairs and into a beautiful and brilliantly decked out little girls' bedroom.

Ginny flopped on the bed and whispered "choo choo," while Athena shot back, even more quietly, "choo choo." The two went back and forth for a while, trying to say the words more and more quietly, until Ginny almost felt like she was hearing Athena's thoughts.

She thought that this might be what happened to best friends after a while. And there seemed to be nothing magical about it. When you know someone, really know someone, maybe it's like a direct phone line into their brain.

When they were together, it seemed like neither girl touched a toy, or drew a picture, or turned on the television. They didn't need to. The world was a toy. And everything around them was amusing. Ginny felt bad for anyone who didn't have their own Athena in their life. She watched her dance now, across the room, and applauded with each turn. She stood up to dance, as well. This was one more thing she could only do because of Athena. And she spun around, hoping this would go on forever.

There was a knock at the door that startled the girls for a moment. A kind-looking man in a beard and a sweater stood at the door.

"Oops, sorry. I just wanted to tell you your mom is making dinner. And it looks pretty good"

From the kitchen, Ginny could hear a higher pitched voice, friendly but demanding, "And no imaginary friends at the dinner table, sweetheart…"

Ginny shared a brave smile with Athena

She looked down at her hand as it started to fade from view. She held back a sigh and hugged her knees, waiting to disappear altogether for a time, just as she always did whenever Athena's mom used the "i" word, wondering where she might go this time.

41 - The I-90 Wormhole

Ironically, Samantha's little red Hyundai was the very first car to pass through the wormhole one side of which was located off the Montrose entrance for the 1-90 Expressway southbound, as she was heading to her therapist, Linda's office.

This is worth mentioning because Linda had been clear with her, the week before, that Samantha needed to become better at taking credit for things when necessary.

Like that time at work when she absolutely had finished not just her part of the new business sales pitch powerpoint, but also the part reserved for finance, and then, on her own, ported the entire thing to google slides for the benefit of the client. There was no award awaiting her at the end of that day. Just a pitch done well that nearly everybody in the entire office had taken credit for.

Except Samantha.

She sighed a bit and leaned over to the notepad tacked to the dashboard of her Hyundai. Linda would want her to write that one down, for their next conversation.

Last week, they had spent nearly the entire session talking about that first time, at the wormhole. Samantha explained that she was late for their weekly visit by nearly two hours because of the wormhole.

She had left home at the right time, for sure. And had picked up a Starbuck's refresher. A strawberry one. Then, to take back a little time, she tried to merge onto the expressway at Montrose, instead of Irving

Park, as she might have otherwise. And that, as they say, made all the difference.

Driving up the ramp she noticed a shimmer in the air, as though a ring of liquid had been tossed up by a giant bucket and had hung there, waiting for the camera to resume to fall to the ground.

Except it didn't fall. And Samantha was too invested in her strawberry refresher to veer aside as the car sunk into the wormhole as it might into any other vertically displayed puddle of water.

In seconds, that vertical puddle had dropped her car in the middle of Shaumburg, far from her therapist's office, but, coincidentally, just minutes from her sister's small yet meticulously decorated bungalow.

Samantha was troubled, scared, late, yet, still...

Well, amazed.

She reached out to the city, obviously, because this was practically what 311 was invented for. And they soon came to investigate it. A perfectly stable wormhole.

In the intervening few months, the fervor had calmed down a bit. Researchers from all over had had the chance to investigate and learn from it.

And that, thought Samantha, shifting in the front seat as she surveyed the traffic, was that.

While Samantha neared the glistening entrance for the wormhole, she took note of the fact that the toll had increased to fourteen dollars and made a slight tsk noise under her breath, fishing for dollar bills at the bottom of her purse and shaking her head at the prospect of being late to see her sister.

42 - In Every Bubble a Word

Leo used the tools on the bubble to draw his perfect woman, lingering on the subtler design process of the genitals far longer than he had spent on any other part, save the face.

Unlike most users, Leo liked to vary the features of the face dramatically each time he conjured up a sex partner from the bubble sitting in his ample bedroom. The Bubble was expensive, and each use sent his power bill skyrocketing beyond the abilities of most citizens to pay.

He joked with friends that each sex partner pulled from the bubble cost the equivalent of a car, but it was a smoother ride. Most had heard Leo say that on a number of occasions, mostly when he canceled engagements, get-togethers, parties, etc, in order to play with his bubble partners. They mostly smiled and walked away quickly. There was no stigma anymore in using temporary 3d printed sex dolls but still, Leo himself was, well...

He was mostly unlikable.

In fact, looking into Leo's eyes was much like looking into the eyes of a shark. No life, no kindness, no emotion stared back at you.

Leo was a shark.

Sharklike, he turned to activate the woman he had spent most of the day designing. She would be sensitive, he knew, because that made it so much better.

And beautiful.

The Bubble whirred to life, randomizing around Leo's design. He rarely had the imagination to name his consorts, so the Bubble itself chose the name Emony, which, had Leo been 40% less shark-like, would have resonated as a beautiful name.

Emony stepped out of the wet glaze of the machine and stood there, naked and defenseless. Leo had had done his best to ensure that his electronic escorts looked as naked and without cover as possible.

Leo reached for her and grabbed Emony between the legs, pulling her closer so he could whisper in her ear. He asked her name, listening to the newly manufactured sound of her voice as she responded. laughing at his toy with a name.

"presumptuous" he thought. "To have a name"

Servos in the Bubble kicked in, following the two figures as Leo marched Emony to his bed. Lights around the electronic panel stirred to life watching as it had happened over and over.

This was the part where Leo would force himself on the woman, telling her over and over she wasn't real, that she was an artifact of his design. She would cry, try to break free, all the while dissolving into the proto matter she was made from.

Except for this time. Leo looked down and saw his hand fall to the floor, sinking into the soft proto-matter goo. There was no way to tell how many times until this trauma caused the bubble to spark a life of its own. To birth someone real who could fight back.

Emony stepped away from the puddle and slipped a shirt on her slight frame.

Her eyes were blue and kind.

43 - In Sight of the Gods

Much like the people all around us, we give the gods power when we believe in them. And we don't need to sell our souls all at one time. It happens gradually, piece by piece. And, eventually the gods claim us as a follower.

Joy, art and music, food, motherhood, money, the gods of each claim us and we fall in line, following our hearts and making them pregnant with power, the power to light up the heavens.

August was an artist. His paintings filled the walls of so many elegant buildings across his native Philadelphia. And when Orin was born, so tiny and beautiful, It was to Apollo that August gave all his thanks. Unseen to August and his family, Apollo accepted this belief, this power, this gratuitous energy, from an artist in celebration of his beloved son, and planned with all his godly directive, for Orin to be an artist ten times more renowned than August himself was.

Apollo was a giving and just god. He loved to laugh. He loved nothing more than to carry out the will of his followers in brightness and beauty, helping them make their own corners of the world into vast patinas of brilliance.

We often think of Heaven as a place because we believe we can FEEL it. But heaven is a state- the state of wallowing in the attention of the gods. Heaven is when you shine so brightly, they can't look away. And as Apollo stared down at Orin, it was not hard for him to think of himself as being in heaven. At one, he was beloved of everyone in his building. By the age of five, he was beloved of the entire neighborhood.

And had caught the errant attention of everyone. Even those that August would have preferred look the other way.

The man with the mole on his face lived down the block from August, and had for years. If anyone on the block had bothered researching the various offender databases, they might have found his picture, and name, atop each one. He had escaped prosecution on more than one occasion, freeing himself from police custody, just to reach out and offend again.

He was a man looked after by no gods, a man who had to use stealth and cunning to invent his own luck. And he did.

August was sure of it.

Even though the police could find no sign he'd taken Orin, the child's father knew. He knew the man with the Mole knew exactly where his boy was. As the weeks wore on, the police became less and less hopeful, while August became more and more desperate, abandoning art, joy, everything good in his life, for the chance to see the child again.

And as August removed the man's fingers, a simple prayer slipped from his lips, praying that Ultio would guide him to find his son. And just like that, Orin became a follower of the goddess of pain and torture.

44 - Infinite in Nature

Christina woke up to the familiar rumblings in her belly that called her, from bed, to the quiet spaces of her bathroom. Flicking on the light, she pulled down the joggers she had fallen asleep in last night, aiming deftly at the gleaming white seat behind her. A regular young lady, she began to flip through her to-do list, noting how this day would look much like any other day.

The satisfying rush of matter from her behind introduced today like it did so many days before. She considered in her head how she would prepare her morning coffee and the scents that awaited her in the nearby shower - much like any other day.

She reached behind her to trigger the flush that usually ended her daily ablutions when a shifting in her stomach encouraged her to remain seated. Another round of waste was evacuated, affording Christina the chance to fall into a unique kind of revelry about her place in the universe, goals for the year, and even how she might thank her building superintendant for the obviously superior functioning of the plumbing, called to her attention by yet a third wave of wet indulgence pouring from her backside like a Flint, Michigan chemical run outside a government sponsored waste treatment plant.

Inhaling quickly, she pushed, participating in the evacuation like she rarely did as the stream intensified, showing no sign of abatement. Her sphincter began to open in ways she hadn't experienced since that experimental party at the home of her ex-boyfriend- the one with the larger than average hands, while she found her concentration broken by an inner alarm that was altogether new.

Well-trained in quantum mathematics, she began to consider spaces within her tiny 5' 4" 110 pound frame and the square footage of waste delivered to her sewer system with each of her increasingly frequent flushes.

"God," she whispered under her breath, "I'm like a poop TARDIS!" an exclamation which set her mind racing on the consequences of this internal vs. external size disparity. Handle slippery with the sweat that began to run from her clammy hands, she imagined the infinity of fecal matter swirling like a remote galaxy within her belly. Her consciousness began to explore the idea, forcing her to stare at herself from a distance, severing her bond with her spiritual self and considering the panoply below her.

The lights in the room intensified, and white subway tile expanded, in front of her, to become a latticework bowing and buckling under the gravity well of her expulsions. Numbers danced in the sclera of her eyes, prophesying the moment when inside and outside of her reached infinity and she became one with a transcendent universe.

For the second time, Christina awakened, floating in a white space she knew instinctively was of her own design. She reached down and pulled up her joggers, trying to get her bearings in an infinity of white space. This universe was untouched, pristine.

And hers to poop in.

45 - The Invisible Man Returns

"Dad, did you get the chocolate chips?" Ayeesha yelled out, still engaged in hand-to-hand combat with her little sister over the ratty yarn-haired doll that bounced between them.

"I sure did. And let your sister have Poppie, ok? There are like 600 other dolls upstairs."

"What?"

"Let your sister have the - you know what? Nevermind. Breakfast!"

The two girls came running, dropping the doll in the hallway. They slid onto stools around the white formica kitchen island looking down hungrily at the pancakes on their plates.

"Thank you, daddy."

Leon put a couple of glasses of milk down near the food, arranging the countertop deftly to look as civilized as possible. Because it had to start that way. The butter and syrup were arrayed in a way that left them immediately accessible to the girls' tiny arms, in amounts that were sensible for their little hands.

This was not Leon's first breakfast.

"Daddy, can you tell us a story while we eat?" Aleata, his youngest, loved to hear stories at all times and Leon loved the way her brain constantly wrapped itself around the narratives. She was a little sponge, in reality. He smiled.

Ayeesha spoke up, "Daddy, tell us about the invisible man."

The girls squealed as Leon launched into a new story of the invisible man. He began with a tiny bit of backstory, about how, when he was younger, his skills at disguise and misdirection rendered him virtually invisible when he wanted to be, unable to be noticed, found, or caught.

He continued on, telling them about a case where he had been sent to investigate a robbery at a museum. Using his skills, Leon faded into the background, looking to all the world like just another art-loving guest. Under the umbrella of his cover, Leon was able to hunt down the thief, discovering, along the way, why it had been so hard to solve this particular heist.

"Why was that, Daddy?" Ayeesha's face was covered in chocolate. Leon's first instinct was to wipe it off, but a part of him realized how little time he had left with them at this age, an age that left them less hyper-conscious about their appearance. He smiled.

"Well, baby girl," he continued. "None of it made any sense because the museum had been robbed by two separate teams on the same day- teams that knew nothing about the other one. Once the two discrete heists were separated, each was easily solved. But before then, it was just a mess of conflicting plans and techniques."

The girls must have found that explanation acceptable. They cheered. "Yay, daddy saves the day"Leon smiled and started cleaning up the count er. He realized that they were half-patronizing him and that was ok. It was fun. He heard footsteps on the stairs.

"Mom's up" he started.

Maya walked in and kissed him widely on the lips. "Are they listening?"

Leon looked wistful. "You know they don't notice me at all when they're like this."

46 - Jump

The brisk Manhattan air chilled Bill's face as his mind wandered to his mother. He didn't blame her for leaving his dad. In truth, he was a small man, uninteresting, unassuming. He blamed her for HOW she left; without demonstration, without confirmation.

She left without showing him how it worked.

Oh, she had told him all about it - how she travelled all over the world, without a boat, without a plane.

Without any help at all.

And she had looked at him and told him he was just like her. They were different. They were a new species- Homo Locus Moventus, and the world, such as it was, belonged to them.

From the tips of pyramids to deep under the earth in faraway caves, secret rooms with no doorways that only our special abilities could enter, deep pockets of civilization under the ocean only available to our kind- to people like us- she had been everywhere.

And one day, he would, too.

Bill listened to her stories and dreamed, and hoped, and wished for the abilities she magically attributed to both of them. Sometimes it seems like his mom forgot that he hadn't done it yet. He didn't know how to, And it wasn't from lack of trying. Nearly every night of his young life, Bill had closed his eyes tensely and imagained, thought of a location, fixated on a spot on the globe, or a place he'd been, or something.

Most recently, he imagined her location. To see himself right next to her. Travelling with her. Visiting her world.

She had explained to him that her abilities had manifested when she fell in front of an oncoming train. Apparently, she said, for our people, the body must absolutely believe it's going to die. It must be convinced completely. And then, once the body is secure that there is no other way, the first time happened. And you found yourself somewhere else. Somewhere safe.

After that, it was like a switch in your brain, one you could flip whenever you needed. But that first time...

Bill researched death. No one had successfully survived a fall over 40 stories. Or 40 minutes underwater, or a massive overdose of barbituates. He even considered his mom's approach- to fall in front of a train, But would his body be ABSOLUTELY convinced he would die? She didn't.

It was a complex issue. Mostly theoretical. Until last night when he looked out his window and saw her, his mother, slowly swinging in the back yard. As he ran out, her body seemed to fold in a direction he'd never seen. And quickly, she got smaller in some dimension he couldn't put his finger on, and she was gone.

And it captivated Bill all night. He imagined this as an invitation. One long waited for.

Where she might be now was what went back and forth through Bill's brain as he closed his eyes and stepped from the roof, slowly counting to 40 under his breath.

47 - The Last Days of the Jackal

You had to admit, when you walked into the room, that this was the chair you would sit in. It was thick and sort of japanese looking and covered in black velvet that appeared to be self-cleaning, if you can say that.

Because it was spotless.

It was just stuffed enough to look ideal, comfortable, not so much as to seem hard to get out of. A simple push and you'd be standing.

This was the comfy chair.

It also stared directly into the doorway, right at the door that opened to the street.

The Jackal had let himself into Lina's house and chosen to sit here for optimum effect. He held the file in his lap, a folder containing all the information needed to kill her husband.

Lina had her reasons. Just as every other person who had come to the Jackal over the last four years had theirs. He was dull. He was loud. He was embarrassing. He was rich but petty.

None of them had ever seen his face, the Jackal. They had contacted him through the dark web, communicated on burner devices with voice changers, and exchanged payment over the most obscure of cryptocurrencies. The Jackal had kept hidden, in secret, a rumor more than anything else, since he had begun this work.

He thought, leaning into the soft facade of the comfy chair, that many people who had gotten into this line of work had done it for the reasons he had. He considered how many just really wanted to know the realities of what was behind the eyes of the people he met every day. Who are these people? What are they willing to do to get what they want.

The Jackal wasn't without sympathy. But his tended to span the entire dynamic, from one side to the other. After all, he himself was often dull. Doing the research needed to explore the dark web certainly hadn't made him any less so. He, himself was sometimes loud, and had been since college. He liked people, ironically, and it made him effulgent, open. Embarrassing, even, sometimes.

And even though he might fight back against the idea that he was petty, at this point, he surely was rich. And hidden enough to get away with a lot. Even, on occasion, finding alternate ways to approach a job.

Let's face it. On more than one occasion. Because the Jackal had a heart. Even if it had been broken. He suspected most people in his line of work had their hearts broken at least once, and tried to put it behind him.

The Jackal took in a deep breath that smelled, more than anything, like Lina. She was a beautiful woman, and she did smell good. He tried to focus on this.

Lina opened the door and immediately realized that the sirens she had heard down the block were meant for her as her gaze hit her husband's eyes, sitting, holding a manilla folder, in the comfy chair.

48 - The Little Things

....

"It's an arms race. It's been like that throughout history." the doctor patted his arm through the biosuit. Doctor Kim had been the only one in this timeline who was even remotely kind to Brannich, although he couldn't find it in him to blame anyone.

"It isn't your fault, really." Doctor Kim packed his bag and moved to the vast array of beakers and tubes splayed out across the table.

"But I have to pay for it." he said, almost under his breath, The doctor snorted and shook his head in resignation,

I mean, someone HAD to pay for it.

The arms race he was talking about was the race between common everyday Viruses and the human immune system. Viruses bred to become ever more invasive and effective in taking down their prey, while humans built up tolerances, daily, monthly, yearly, and powered on.

On their side, the viruses had a powerfully fast generative cycle, allowing them to be generations ahead of their hosts. While humans had the strength of their minds, creating anti-toxins and vaccines that helped them speed up their viral response, fighting back the way they knew how.

Or that's how he had learned it in school.

Today was October 15th, and it was clear that the timestream had no interest in joining mankind's fight against the tiny virus.

Ten days ago, on the 5th, in another timeline, Brannich stepped into the time machine as a test. His intention was to go back 5 years into the past and then spend an uneventful day, returning to his very moment of departure a hero, the man who had plumbed the secrets of time.

But the chain of events had gone absolutely differently. The very day he arrived, people began dropping dead, all around him. He stayed on to try to fix things.

The intervening 5 years had passed with Brannich watching almost a third of the population of the planet die. And the changes seemed permanent. Not even the fact that he didn't go back in this timeline matterred. People kept dying.

They quarantined him, but it was too late. They destroyed his machine but that did nothing. They even found the version of him in this timeline and summarily executed him, in hopes he would be prevented from going back.

Nothing worked. Not one thing.

Doctor Kim coughed up blood this time as he muscled past Brannich to leave through the airlock door. Brannich yelled after him, asking him what he should do now? Brannich himself was no epidemiologist. He was powerless to stop this problem that he had started, when he stepped into the past with a 5-year more advanced version of the common flu virus.

The doctor turned, "Kim. It is my name. Remember." and then he filed out, without looking back.

Brannich made a mental note now. Over the last few weeks he had been given so many names to remember. So many people to mourn when he was the last man on earth.

49 - Magic

Anais' parents threw away her first letter from the far-away wizarding school. They believed that it was not a good fit, and tossed it away in the trash before she could even see it.

But, as the letters came with greater frequency, it became clear that this was a matter requiring some attention. The letters were relentless, urgent, pleading to be opened.

In some cases, outright demanding it.

This was clear to her parents one Saturday morning when a flock of birds descended on their small Surrey home, slipping through open windows, down chimneys and, in one case, through a crack in the basement, each holding a thin and yellowed letter in their tiny beak.

Soon, her parents gave in, and Anais sat in her room, tearing away the red wax bond that sat across the parchment flap, and read:

"Anais Tolerun," You are humbly invited to attend classes at Marigrave school for Witchcraft and Wizardry on this, the 23rd day of July, 2022, for the upcoming semester. Please respond to us with your availability and willingness to become a Marigrave Witch."

For ten year old Anais, this was not just an introduction into the mysteries of magic but also a personal message from the universe - the first of its kind- that she existed, as an individual, a person who was unique and her own person.

It was possibly the first piece of mail ever addressed to her.

This made the note nearly impossible to ignore, as she ran to the kitchen table where she traditionally had done her homework to pen a response. Her parents looked sadly at her hunched back in the frosty afternoon light and thought only about the many ways she could be hurt, but physically and emotionally.

It went without saying that they had different plans for their daughter.

And months later, it almost seemed like a different Anais who sat attentive in class in the dimly lit grandeur of Marigrave castle. She was confident, powerful, aware of things that had been only stories to her last year, from books she had long outgrown.

She breathed in the slightly aromatic air of the castle, filled with herbs and remnants of potions and tried to identify each scent as she was called by a faraway voice to the front of the classroom.

Lifting her robes from the floor, she stepped onto the stone floor, fingering the tiny chunk of metal in her pocket. She looked over at Roemy and Michael, the other members of her coven, and they urged her on lovingly. Much like her parents, they had never let the fact that Anais was born without magical abilities change how they felt about that partnership - or that love.

Reaching the front of the room, she picked up the 3-foot-long radio controlled car and snapped the 9 volt battery into the open slot on the bottom, smiling as the tiny purr of the engine drew oohs and ahs from the witches and wizards in the room.

50 - Magic Loom

November 27th, 2024: Daniel Vath, founder of Magic Loom, is killed by a small crowd of fanatics outside his New York Condo.

November 25th, 2024: A dramatic stock market crash causes the country to fall into chaos. Riots break out in the street and many people die. The Riots spread across all big cities.

November 17th, 2024: Herculon, the primary hero of washington DC, battles Virago in the pool in front of the Washington monument. Virago catches him from behind with his left arm, covered in razor sharp spikes, and impales him through his Magic Loom supersuit. Herculon dies slowly on camera, causing stock in Magic Loom, the only textile company catering exclusively to superheroes, to plummet.

June 1st, 2022: Herculon updates his dated costume with the help of Sintec designs in Seattle who outsource all textiles to Magic Loom, a corporation in Veritas, Texas, renowned for making indestructible materials

May 13th, 2022: A freedom of information act lawsuit stalls as Marchiotta Fabrics fails to obtain the secret material ingredient in Magic Looms famous "Hero first" uniform material.

January 2nd, 2021: At a meeting of the Infinity Union, The Rapture, hero of the people of Utah makes fun of Herculon's uniform, calling him out for its dated color and cut.

August 15th, 2020: The new issue of GQ is released, including a cover shot of The Rapture, calling him the best dressed male hero, focusing on the deep green and blue of his uniform, cut perfectly to show off his physique.

August 3rd, 2015: Herculon arrives in Washington, a hot new hero, vying to be the top superhero in the city.

March, 15th, 2000: Magic Loom stores materials spun for the last 13 years in a large lofted warehouse in Seatlle for use by its subsidiaries, including the design firm, Sintec designs.

May 23rd, 1995: The NYPD gives up on over a hundred cases of missing men and women, claiming no reasonable leads and a paucity of manpower.

July 25th, 1992: Kelly disappears from the assembly line. She has no family and is not close with many people.

July 15th, 1992: Kelly's immediate supervisor, Howard, follows her into the employee bathroom and rapes her, explaining to her that she can tell no one or run the risk of losing her job.

June 20th, 1992: Kelly settles in to Magic loom, working in the assembly area, helping to mold the material for Magic Loom's "Hero First" fabric, sold as invulnerable to all attacks.

June 3rd, 1992: Kelly is hired to work at Magic Loom after a lengthy interview process. A subsequent exam, paid for by Magic Loom, reveals that her hymen is intact.

August 30th, 1987: Daniel's company, Magic Loom, Goes public with an IPO that tops 30 million dollars.

July 20th, 1980: Daniel Vath finds reference to a magical loom that will spin invulnerable material from the blood of a virgin in the back of an old alchemy text. He spends over a million dollars and five years finding it.

51 - Melting Point

3 seconds: Professor Zed, the Mind Eater, speculated, back in the 60s, that the temperature needed to destroy the Grey Guardian was about 60,000 degrees, sustained for 20 seconds He devoted the last 10 years of his life to creating that temperature and eliminating his nemesis, coming close in 1975, when his rain of giant globe lightning killed 40 people, almost killing the Guardian himself.

Almost.

The Grey Guardian survived and stopped his plan, saving millions. Still, those 40 people hung heavily on him. The Guardian had a deep commitment to life and had never killed. It was hard for him not to bear those 40 on his shoulders. They died because of him. He believed

Ironically, The professor had a change of heart during his lifetime prison sentence and had shared his data with the Grey Guardian- what he had learned about the hero's mortality and limits.

Often, the Guardian missed the simplicity of that time.

4 seconds: As the Grey Guardian grew older, he seemed physically unchanged. His hair was still a shock of black riding high atop his head. He still filled his costume out with wide shoulders and seemingly effortlessly cut musculature. The only place you could see his age was in his eyes. Eyes that were almost 70 years older.

If, however, you shared his molecular-vision, able to distinguish energies in the nano range, you would see other differences, as every year the Guardian got stronger - harder to hurt. The alien energies that made him into a superhero were still at work, every day, aging him into a god. A god who currently floated, almost casually, in the corona of the sun.

5 seconds: The Guardian hung, unbuffeted by the 2,000,000 degree solar winds as he considered time. The newly extrapolated estimates of his abilities suggested he could survive 10 seconds at this temperature before his diamond hard skin cracked and melted from his frame. To his exponentially sped up cognition and senses, however, 10 seconds was a lifetime to think- to deliberate. And he did.

6 seconds: He returned, as he did nearly every second, to the moment where he had made the decision to stop Kuchin, the dictator threatening to blow up the nation of Laos. The Grey Guardian had used his ever-expanding abilities and peered into the young leader's mind, finding a committed, engaged sociopath who would not stop until the world was subjugated under him. In that split second, staring into the brain of a man who would be the next Hitler, he made a choice.

And he turned him off.

7 seconds: The Guardian considered that choice. Given a lifetime to think, he would be unable to choose otherwise. The threat was too severe- too extreme. Kuchin did what he felt he had to. And so had he.

8 seconds: Considering time, the Guardian knew that today he could die, but was unsure if the same was true tomorrow. And the next two seconds stretched into eternity

52 - The Mig

There was nothing on the ground in Anniko's way across the sanctuary floor for at least a thousand meters so she let herself relax as she walked, reaching out only casually with her hands in front of her to find secure footing.

She tried to use the Mig's sacred language for all of it while she walked, but in her head, she cheated a little. She knew that a meter was almost 5 q'mars - nearly the height of an average person, and this let her visualize it more easily.

Anniko let the calumn bells ring in her head, marking off the time, and she realized she might be early. She slowed down her steps so much, her foot pads began to classify and catalogue the healing plants under her, the gifts of the earth that had bounced back with such a fervor from the scorched wind.

The Larok people relied on the gifts of the earth and had suffered when they disappeared. But since the Mig had landed three years ago, the ground had given back again, had partnered again with Anniko's people, providing security. They, in turn, had given the Mig his due worship, despite the sickly pink of his skin and the gangly raw stretched out form he walked about in, towering over the Larok people and looking, all the time, as though he might break or collapse, folding in two before he fell.

The Mig explained about monsters- the things that helped people and made their lives easier. He painted such a beautiful picture in their minds of this monster that he was building, enlisting the help of people all over the teneb to build it.

Anniko had been grateful to help. And would be again. In her head, the monster would stand up and use his immense power to make all their lives better, Not just the pink Mig, but also all the blues across the planet, the Larok, living peacefully, in hope for the future.

She came closer to the end of the sanctuary, stepping into the land that had been given to the Mig for all his help and support. The plants grew wild here, out of control, free, love drunk with the foul material the Mig poured on them a number of times a day. She was reminded of what Elder Curell had said, asking her if she meant to believe her nose, or the joy of the plants.

She believed the plants.

She smelled the rotten sweet fruit smell of the Mig, himself, as she bowed toward him, thinking him again in all three of the Larok languages for the ground's strong crop. She might have spoken a little louder than usual, a little more sonorous, in anticipation of sacrificing her voice to the monster he was building much as she had sacrificed her eyes some years before.

She wondered what the monster looked like while she tried to make her last words sound gracious and thankful.

She hoped it was blue.

53 - Mint Condition

Red poured through the items on the counter, one at a time, imagining he could feel the actor's energy, even now. It was always tough to figure out what was a real file and what was just a charlatans's tossed away piece of junk.

"You feel that?" Asked the store owner, invading his reverie.

"Hm?"

"It's like you can feel their energy sometimes, their spirit."

"Except he's still alive." Red did some quick math in his head.

The store owner laughed.

"Yes, right, for sure. He is. But I always think I can image I feel, well, something. It really is real. It belonged to him."

And that was true

His genspanner showed that not only was this filled with the real targets DNA, that it held over 75% of a perfect sequence. And filled in the gaps completely, meaning that, with the 5 other files he owned, Red could build a full sequence.

It was real.

The store owner, a doughy, bearded man in his 50s, went on, " I mean, I like a lot of his early work, but a lot of that gets overshadowed."

He went to reach out again for the cigarette case, with the monogram RDJ emblazoned in gold across the front. Red was quicker.

"I'll take it.".

He pulled it carefully from the counter into the green plastic specimen bag, waiting for the wash of solvents to deliver the DNA sequences to the spanner housing. As red passed the cash to him directly, he silently tracked the lineage of the 20 ten dollar bills, pulling them from the uppermost slots in this hybrid wallet.

Red was a professional. The store owner was effulgent and invited him to look through the rest of the dull, shapeless items owned at one time or another by someone famous. Red was uninterested. He had what he'd come for.

Red had been a collector for almost 20 years now. And he was good. Maybe the best. Probably because, in the dangerous, lucrative, and highly illegal collector's world he lived in, he didn't do it for the money.

He slid out the front door and backtracked to the alley. Rifling through the garbage cans, he found a small black paper bag. He pulled the case from its green sleeve and placed it in the bag, along with the excess bills he had picked up here. The only thing he would take with on this trip home was information: a series of Cs, TS, ga, and as.

The black bag dropped to the ground as Red dissolved in a vertical puddle of blue. The gray sheen of his home work space nearly 200 years forward from where he'd stood wrapped around him.

Red took a breath and pressed "go" on the linear age function. He was in now 100%. Once he had aged the clones, he would have a pristine set of the 5 primary stars of the biggest grossing film series of the 21st century. Perfect. In their boxes.

Mint condition.

54 - Modern Medicine

Kono felt a bit heavy, leaden, this morning and wasn't sure why, almost as if he were tied to the bed, or had a weight placed on his chest. It wasn't a comfortable feeling.

He slid out from an opening on the side, where the mound of coverlets and pillows were slightly less piled high and deep. He kicked a pillow in annoyance and it came down against the frame of a light in the far side of the corner, which fell over clattering against the wall before it disappeared, integrated back into the flowing omniwalls of his spacious room.

This was a C- morning at best, he considered. And that made him laugh a little, rounding out his temper. The walls behind him consumed the bed as well as he stepped into the space in the corner where the bathroom generally manifested. He lifted his penis from his shorts to urinate as a small opening appeared, on command, from the area where the wall and floor met. It felt heavy in his hands, as well- meaty and large.

That thought made him consider masturbating at least once, before going about the day. This would be a complicated day with very little time to himself and likely no time to explore this part of himself.

He held his penis in one hand now and made a sly, come hither look to the wall, shimmering to life as a morning mirror. It was all so absurd that the thought of jerking himself off, sweaty, pounding, in the corner while the day moved on around him seemed less satisfying than silly

He already knew there were no clothes for him in any of the room's compartments, but, luckily, the silver package had arrived yesterday with his work clothes. Today was going to be an experience that was a bit outside the everyday for Kono. He was tired already just considering how his one day out of the year of menial labor would feel tomorrow when he was back by the pool, or hiking. Or running laps around his opulent home.

But modern life required some sacrifice

Before he forgot, he fished the case from the servodrawer in the wall, pulling out a giant greenish white horsepill and placing it on the tiny shelf next to him that had quickly ramped out from the wall. He shook his head automatically at the size of it.

He could never take these things without water, no matter what his throat was shaped like, and today was no different. He imagined gagging on the oblong pill, damning modern medicine in his head. The Omniwalls served up a cup of cool water.

But as the pill made its way down his throat he lightened up. He tucked himself back into his shorts one more time and reminded himself that even though it hurt his gullet a bit to swallow, at least by this time tomorrow he would be female again and maybe not so annoyed about it.

55 - Monkey Paw Pt. 2

Amanda fingered the small, desiccated paw in her hand for almost an hour before she knew, with any degree of certainty, what her wish would be.

I mean, she knew how monkey paw wishes worked. And there was nothing really wrong with her life as it was. It might not be worth it to risk misfortune for some wish that she might not even need.

She leaned back into bed and kissed the back of the man lying to the left of her. Appreciating the symmetry of the situation, she leaned over and placed a small kiss on the forehead of the man to her right as well. A small, but not inconsequential wish that bubbled up, almost to the surface was that they might wake up soon and continue the barbaric triad they had accomplished last night over and over again.

Thinking back, Amanda could understand why they were still sleeping and it brought a small smile to her face. She wasn't a man-killer - more like a man exhauster.

Women, too, come to think of it.

And that thought brought her back to the monkey's paw. Miles and Jonathan. They were really adorable. And dear to her. She couldn't stomach the idea that some ambient, poorly considered wish on her part might hurt them in any way.

Or Gina, or Marcus, or Zelinda, Parish, any of the people she regularly brought into her bed and felt close to. What a horrible thing if her wishes caused them any distress. The thought almost made her toss the Monkey's paw away. No wish was worth hurting any of them.

Even the random people she met and played with. The tall, aristocratic looking guy at Margo's last week who had the nerve to ask her for sex in the bathroom. She loved thinking about the incredulous look in his eyes while he was inside her on the bathroom sink. She loved saying yes and feeling the warm glow of accomplishment from new friends.

Or the girl in the glasses who tried to explain how Magic the gathering worked last wednesday. The more she explained, the hotter she got, until Amanda's tongue was suddenly tickling her armpits in her sparse Logan Square bedroom. Amanda wanted her to just keep talking forever, between tiny bites and kisses. But please talk some more.

She sighed and sunk into that thought as it occurred to her what she might wish for.

Amanda was 102 years old when she died, surrounded by a throng of friends and family, including four particularly doting great grandchildren, one of whom couldn't be torn away from her bedside even hours later. She slipped away quietly in her opulent home on her custom made bed with 800 thread count Egyptian silk sheets at 11:24 pm, just moments after she considered, in a slight but intense flurry of concern, that there could be some downside to this wish, that she would get one hundred dollars every time someone called her a slut.

56 - My Trunk

....

The universe asks big questions sometimes.

Like why do I need a million dollars? I mean, sure, I want a million dollars.

But why did I need it?

The thing you aren't going to believe, as I'm writing this, is that the trunk didn't give me any answers, or conclusions, no great insights into the world, nothing.

Except what I needed.

And to be clear, that's what I had sussed out on my own.

So when I opened the trunk that first time and pulled out $1,000,234.20 it turns out that this was exactly, to the penny, what I needed to pay off my taxes, pay my debts, and buy the house.

And after living in my car for two months, I needed that house.

So there it began, and it continued, just about once a week. I would open the trunk of my small red civic and would be greeted by something I needed. Once it was a ladder, needed to fix a window on the side of the house. Once I found a bag of unopened chinese food, egg foo yung, some white rice, enough to keep me going all night when I was sick as a dog. .

Clothing, socks, a new blanket. Once it was a water resistant jacket on a cloudy day. But it's not always that easy to figure out.

I

mean, the can of Narcan was easy enough to make sense of. And the 36 pack of water as I drove to Ohio for rehab.

But it was sometimes a challenge. I didn't realize I needed a decent pair of shoes until I pulled them out of the trunk, tried them on, and they fit. Better than the raggedy converse I so often wore. And I was completely perplexed by the gun.

The gun appeared three weeks ago. Originally, I was afraid to touch it. I'd never been near a gun before. But after a week it was clear it wasn't going anywhere. I realized I would just be driving around with it in my trunk if I didn't take it in so I did. I placed it in the top drawer of my dresser in my bedroom. And never touched it again. I know how this works, though. And I know you'll find it there.

There are big and small questions. I realize I've been conditioned to look for opportunities. And I will find them. Whatever force is delivering to me what I need, I know I can take these things and make sense of them.

So, for me, the big question, as I finish this confession here today, is not, "Did I kill her?" or "Why did I murder someone I don't even know?" It's a question of whose body this is that was pulled out of my trunk during that police stop, who really killed her, and why, really, why, does the universe think I need to be in Jail?

And now is when I sign my name.

57 - Nana Buruku

Nana Buruku's beautiful back mane seemed to nearly reach the water as she leaned over the side of the ship in her invocation to Mami Watta. On her own, she was strong enough to do whatever she needed, but she was never alone. Her fellowship with the Ocean spirit filled her head with possibilities, and gave her kinds of strength she hadn't even considered.

She felt the power wash over her as the night air brushed her skin with an affection only her gentle Mawu could demonstrate, soft and graceful, like the reflected light that made all nights into spaces of wonder all over the world.

She looked down and saw a young Igbo boy handing her a thick, fresh fish. He mouthed her name "Olisabuluwa" and smiled with joy. She smiled back and took the fish into her hands. Whispering to it, she released it to the water, where it quickly splashed and swam away. The boy laughed even as his head spun around, keyed to the laughter behind him. The men in the hold called to him as hundreds of fish appeared in the barrels that were often so empty before.

In the dispersed moonlight, a man and a woman came to retrieve the boy, and they stared at her in awe. Nana Buruku smiled and motioned them closer. She was not standoffish or separate. She had joined this ship in order to be with her people, to solve the riddle of where her people had been taken to, and she took joy in their company.

She had been away for too long a time, exploring, and had left the world in the care of Mawu-Lisa, her beloved children. On her bare hands, even now, could be seen, on the left, the tattoo that had called up Lisa, the sun, and on her right, the mark that had originated Mawu, her daughter, the moon.

Across her belly, she wore, similarly, the tattoos that had pulled into existence her precious Legba, the trickster, in men's minds, and the brilliant snake Aido Hwedo, so perfectly attuned to nature. On her breasts and shoulders she wore her lesser children and grandchildren. And in the deep color of her skin, tattooed from head to toe in a rich beautiful ebony, every child of the earth.

More people rose, from the hold, confident that the crew of the ship had gone, disappeared, and that there would be no repercussion. Nana Buruka raised her hand and the ship's rigging was suddenly full of tiny lights, illuminating the deck, lighting up the faces of the people milling around her. She saw Fon and Ewe and Igbo standing all together and laughed to herself as she realized that they were all seeing her differently, a different manifestation.

She recognized a young Yoruba girl, far from her people, and reached out to hold her hand, keeping her company until they eventually reached their destination and Nana Buruku could find out, finally, what was happening to her people.

58 - No Clue

It only took a couple of cases to completely destroy Officer Aranda's reputation. Which wasn't the intent at all. At least I don't think it was.

You could almost say Aranda's entire life was collateral damage.

The whole thing began when Ronnie and Tina were young, in the middle of making discoveries that would guide the rest of their lives.

Tina had discovered that she was good at taking. She was expert at charming, and misdirecting, and building the just-right environment for her to walk off with what she wanted. This skill would eventually propel her into a life of not-so-common thievery.

It would lead her to a penthouse full of what was once owned by the elite and wealthy. Paintings and sculptures, jewelry and rugs, beautiful things that filled the empty spaces for her. But even more beautiful than the goods themselves was the sense of accomplishment she got from walking away free, with everything she could carry.

Every time.

And even though she could never prove it, she suspected, every day, that Ronnie had something to do with that. Ronnie's abilities had grown, too, in ways that she kept secret from everyone, even her sister. Whatever they were, though, they were sufficient to leave Ronnie with the reputation of being someone effective, someone who could make the most of every opportunity...

Someone who succeeded.

And that's how it always looked to me, on the outside.

Despite all that, Ronnie adored her sister. She would do anything for her.

And it turns out, she had.

Now you can take this one case as an example, if you want. Or you can imagine, in your head, that it was the last time, that this was the final time that Ronnie would go to all ends to protect her sister.

But I'm here to tell you, it wasn't.

When Tina broke into the museum that night to steal the small group of paintings that had been taken, themselves, years before, by the nazis and never returned, you can believe that she had good in her heart.

You can believe that she never meant to hurt that young curator, who, despite her schedule, was unfortunately not at dinner.

You can believe that Tina never meant to ruin that young woman's life, Just as Ronnie never intentionally meant to ruin Officer Aranda's.

For all it would get you, you could believe that all day. If you really wanted to.

And today, even Ronnie found it hard to believe that her sister could have done what she saw in front of her, but it changed nothing. This is what she'd done her whole life. She heard the door creak as Aranda started to step through, only seconds behind her, and she was impressed, despite herself.

Not that it mattered. She lifted the bag of cleaning supplies from her back and pressed her eyes shut, concentrating on a single point, just like she had done since she was younger, whenever she wanted to stop time.

59 - One Note

It was all about practice; Investment in his talent, Danny realized, as he laid down a soft, plaintive vocal track. He listened back and could hear the shimmer around his vocals that meant it was working.

It was in high school he noticed that when he shifted to his singing voice, his emotional state seemed tangible, visible, even incandescent.

It was Amy from the dance team who leaned in closely and melted into him. He heard the shimmer. He knew exactly what she was responding to. Her pupils enlarged like saucers, giving her eyes the near-appearance of absolute black metal, glossy and smooth, staring into him while her hands fumbled at the front of his pants whenever she could, mirroring his want, validating his need.

And the effect wasn't lost on Mr. Mcnulty, his math teacher, he found, when he met him after class and began to slowly sing out his apologetic apathy for all things mathematical and desire to be excused from the class forever with an "A." Danny felt stupid beginning the song, but he watched the older man's eyes and saw the lightness and color drain from them, while he tidied up his desk and prepared Danny's transfer papers, with all perfect scores.

Danny dropped his bookbag next to him in the open study class he now enjoyed with Amy. Could it really be this simple? He had found that practicing the emotion in his words, in his tune, created a desired effect on the listener. That's it. It's not magic, it must be just science. And that's what Danny believed. Some notes, coupled with his own mercurial desire seemed to bend the world to his needs. It was no more mysterious than the successes of a great debater or a masterful hypnotist. It was simple. It just wasn't very lucrative.

Despite his talents, Danny had grown up as poor as most of the artists we emulate. It's possible Danny was different, digging deeper, recognizing the injustice of it all. And so when he walked into the bank with a tape recording of his voice, feeling compassionate, feeling like changing the world, all he asked for was the teller to wipe all the records on the computer. Suddenly people struggling with debt for decades were off the hook. Homes owned by the bank were now wholly owned by the people in them. Danny fingered the recorder in his pocket. He could get up on stage now and channel that - convince people everywhere to change it all.

Which is how it started. With an Idea. And it ended in a club.

As his single note scream fed back in a wash across the venue, the eyes of the audience shone black like so many marbles, glinting in the stage strobes while they climbed onto the stage like one liquid organism. Danny could feel the anger he had stoked in waves, but more than that, he couldn't help but realize, as he was ripped apart, he felt their bliss.

60 - One Week

Xandra inherited the little metal cigar box from her girlfriend. Anna had killed herself a few days earlier, but not before she had explained to Xandra how the box worked. It would let the owner send messages back from exactly one week in the future.

Monday: 2am on Monday, the fourth time Xandra had opened the box, it held two pieces of paper. The first was a note in her handwriting that said "You have one week."

The second was a photograph of a gun.

Xandra spent the night crying, missing Anna.

Tuesday: Xandra began the process of taking her life apart. She walked into JJ's office, past her desk where she usually sat, coding, and told him to go jump up his own ass. She quit before he had the presence to fire her and lit the vase full of dead flowers on her old desk on fire as she walked out.

Wednesday: She set up a zoom call with her mother for the morning and one with her father at night. She was sincere, but stern, hanging up when she wanted. She went home and canceled about half her subscriptions, feeling comfortable dying with a Hulu no ads package but not with an unused Amazon Prime account. She watched The Handmaid's Tale's first episode again and the last episodes of 5 more of her favorite shows.

Thursday: She visited the spa and found her high school ex, Rhonda, working the front desk. Rhonda showed her the entire place and set her up with a VIP special. The 600 dollars she had taken out of the bank that morning were no good here, Rhonda laughed. So she asked her to join her in the mudbath and they made out for two hours.

Friday: She looked up two more ex girlfriends, including one, Alisa, who had dated her and Anna together. Alisa was free that night, so she went out for tacos with her, throwing around her 600 dollars like Elon Musk at Radio Shack. She went down on Alisa in the car on the way home and the two of them wrote each other's phone numbers in marker, huge, on their bellies.

Saturday: Xandra gave away everything in her house she hated, including the blue chair that everyone said was by some famous designer. She drove around the city delivering furniture to friends, reconnecting, laughing, and hugging.

She and her friend Margot lit the blue chair on fire that night in a Rosco Village alley. It burned blue, too.

Sunday: Xandra slept on her favorite couch all day.

As the clock rounded 2am, Xandra lifted herself from the couch, exhausted and made her way to the tiny box on her desk. She pulled out the note and photograph, wondering whose gun was in the picture, anyway. She laughed as she opened the box to send them back, seeing a tiny orange piece of paper with 5 numbers on it.

It was probably a good week to win the lottery

61 - Oneday

Stepping out of his front gate for the first time in a year, Niko looked down the block, he saw at least two or three people doing the same and it felt good to be part of a group, even one so separate.

He pulled at his mask and pressed the button that covered the lower part of his face. The sun looked huge today, an optical illusion caused by the gas magnification, but the air seemed temperate, even brisk, whipping around him. The grey wind cones that had threatened to spoil everything were gone and the sky opened, welcoming him.

On his phone, Niko had downloaded his itinerary for the entire day, scouring the city net for just the right occasions, places where he might see just the right number of friends. Not so many that they couldn't occupy the area simultaneously - not so few that they missed conversation that Niko needed right now.

The last OneDay was admittedly a bit of a letdown for Niko, with Mai leaving for another complex and his Uncle, the last of his family, moving to the tunnels. Niko couldn't afford to let this OneDay celebration be anything but perfect.

For the past five years, OneDay had been the most important annual event across the globe, celebrated on a different day each year, and a different day in each country. The combination of severe weather conditions caused by global climate change and ongoing epidemics caused by Neoviruses released by melting ice all over the world had sent everyone deep into their homes waiting for a day, a single day every year, when conditions would align enough to let them walk outside. It was a day to be appreciated

And Niko did

First, to a brunch where he met up with Jonnie, Marisa, and at least five of his friends he'd seen lately only on their regular multi zoom calls. They took every opportunity to brush against each other, each accidental touch a kiss, each casual foot contact below the table a hug, reminding them that they were friends, that they loved each other.

Together, they worked their way across the city, ending with the museum showing Jonnie's art, a singer songwriter in the corner, filling the room with an acoustic version of a Nirvana song that brought the room to tears amidst the bright red paper lanterns Jonnie had patiently built, painted, and lit all across the room.

He had seen Jonnie's sculptures online and at the video premiere, but to see them up close, to touch them. It was a sudden pull at his heart- a deepening pride in his friend's accomplishments, to know they were real,

It was dark by the time he got home, sliding into a warm bath and considering every moment of the day, as a nun might finger a rosary. His wrists slipped below the surface of the reddening water, a color that reminded Niko of one of Jonnie's brilliant fans, lighter than air, carrying you upward.

62 - The Ones Who Feel for the State

The commissioner was a regular visitor at Hope House, despite the fact that he never visited any of the caretakers privately, and seemed to have no use for their services.

Previous commissioners had visited, similarly, and made sure to visit many caretakers, ensuring that the process worked for everyone, that it was fair, that it was joyful, that it made sense.

And since all visits were anonymous, no one knew what these particular visits were about.

Except in the broadest sense, where they were about happiness.

The commission on human happiness was initiated over a decade ago, after the invention of the mindslip. The slip solved a problem for people that had been nagging at humanity since the beginning of time. In a world where happiness was important, what could be done for people who knew, absolutely knew, that they could never be happy.

These were people who found pain in their own existence. Their desire to end that pain often read like a need to end that existence. In the past, so many had committed suicide as a last hope- as a final option.

The mind slip was just a better final option.

If someone decided they wanted to end it, they could surrender themselves to the mind slip. There, skilled technicians would align and adjust the brain, removing the problematic personality, and overwriting it with one that could truly be happy with the skills, interests, and instincts of the body it was housed in.

This had been the model for over ten years, where state-sponsored medical techs made over suicidal people into people who joyfully participated in everything the world had to offer. Many of those people found themselves here, at a local Hope House, where the constant party atmosphere allowed them to exercise their happy instincts in big and profound ways.

Just being a part of this made the commissioner himself happy. On good days, he wondered aloud how many people his organization was able to make truly happy. And even though this methodology was not without detractors, the world mostly agreed.

Which was more than he could say about nearly anything.

The commissioner smiled as he nursed his drink and stared across the room at the beautiful redhead whose laughter infectiously filled the room. She was nude except for a pair of multicolor stockings, holding on tightly to two men taking turns fondling her and kissing her full on the lips.

She seemed happy, inspired, as she teased them both, until they lifted her onto the table and began to penetrate her. There was something light about her, without concern, as she basked in their attention.

He remembered the feel of those lips and wished, just passingly, that she could have been happy in their marriage, recognizing, even as he thought it, that this was, in reality, a different Heather than the one with whom he had exchanged those vows.

He left a tip on the table as he walked off, satisfied that the system worked.

63 - The Only Birthday I Remember

She's not your real daughter, you know," Angelo slid into the booth next to the young girl, his eyes trained on his ex wife.

Miri stared back as the smile fell from her face. She looked down at the empty gift box on the table and fingered the longer-than-necesssry red ribbon. "I don't really come to you when I'm looking for perceptions of reality."

Angelo's daughter was slim and dark haired and quiet in the booth seat next to him. Her eyes were in her lap and her hands out of sight. She looked scared as the waitress came with two milkshakes.

Angelo brushed away Miri's hand and took one from the tray, beginning to drink, handing the other to his daughter. "Please, for this one, if you can bring something diet. Or a water"

"I hope you enjoy that," Miri shot back, once the waitress stepped away.

Angelo leaned in. "It's been five years, bitch. I sent you away five years ago. And now I see you you're too dumb to leave. Birthday presents?" he swatted the empty gift box from the table.

"Adults divorce. You don't throw away children." Miri attempted to match his intensity, but more restrained, more orderly. It infuriated the bigger man.

"You have no business in her life." He pressed his hand down on his daughter's leg. Even if the girl hadn't told Miri, it would have been clear that the abuse had begun. All the reasons why Miri had left had been visited upon the girl. Miri struggled to stay calm.

"I think you will find that you never really understood what my business was," She countered, watching his eyes to see when the small capsule dissolving in his drink would take effect.

"What business? You are in the business of being a pain in my ass." Angelo downed the milkshake with a giant gulp. His daughter looked up and caught Miri's eye. There was compassion to be found there, amidst the embarrassment.

The Waitress returned, carrying a water, for which Miri thanked her. There was no advantage dragging her into all this, but she was doing her part perfectly. Miri left a 20 for the check.

Angelo's slurred words sent the waitress walking off, shaking her head. She was familiar with what kind of trouble a drunken patron could bring. And when the beefy man's head hit the table, it was no surprise. There were only two ways a visit from a drunken customer could end. And the kindest one was head down on the table.

The dark haired girl slipped from behind him, exiting the booth. She held the knife from the gift box with the blade held flat as she had when puncturing Angelo's spine. Later, after they had driven off, she would tell Miri she had done as the woman had taught her, stabbing deeply and firmly into the back of the neck,with the blade point angled toward the front center, firmly yanking the knife towards the spine.

64 - Original Sin

Eve sat crosslegged on a bed of grass and considered what the snake had told her.

The Idea itself was hypnotic, drawing her in and making her feel flush. She wondered why it had never occurred to her before even as she realized that this was the reason for the intoxication she felt. It was so far beyond what she might have invented on her own.

Eve had tried, over the last few months of her life, to give audience to all of the animals, listening intently to their concerns and ideas as she played In the near infinite garden. Even as Adam seemed caught up in his own sense of God given mastery over these creatures, she seemed so much more excited by the possibility of partnership with them - of a kind of union that might satisfy them all.

The minds of these animals seemed unique to her, unusual, even special. She heard the sheep talking about a burgeoning fear they had that they had that their friendship with many of the larger animals would soon come to an end as the physical needs of life in the garden won out over the simplistic ideals that they all seems to live by.

She heard the lions as they bristled under the restrictions that seemed to prevent them from being their best selves - their strongest selves - in a world that perpetually mandated order over their instincts and desires.

She heard the larger animals, wanting a kind of freedom that the garden, as expansive as it was, was ill-equipped to deliver, and she heard the smaller animals as they talked about hiding food for a time that, in their short stint on earth, had yet to ever happen, but gnawed at the edges of their brains like a tiny flame eating away at a leaf.

But it was only the simple serpent who ever listened to her, heard her. The snake asked what she was thinking, sat in quiet while she talked, curious about her fears, desires, instincts. She serpent asked questions, prodded her to reveal herself. And was the only animal willing to give her its own knowledge.

Eve captured Adam's hand in hers, Running her fingers across the smooth, lighter interior of his palm. He really was beautiful, strong, Sun kissed even. A playful smile flashed across her face as she guided him to the tree in the center of the garden.

She leaned back against the trunk behind her and slid down its rough bark, planting her ass into the crook of the old root-woven foot of the behemoth. spreading her legs in the warm afternoon air, she felt drunk with exposure and anticipation.

Eve pulled his head down between her open legs and guided it gently to her core. She closed her eyes as he put his tongue out to taste her, in that place that looked like a perfect apple, split with the utmost care by the expert blade of God's own paring knife.

65 - The Pornographic Man

Zeke leaned back into the overstuffed grey sofa and asked Amelia to take off her bra and touch herself.

"Like this?" the dark haired girl on the screen pulled off her top and pushed back in her chair. She wore only a thin grey pair of socks now and Zeke could see everything.

"God, thank you," Zeke pulled harder at himself now, trying to masturbate, trying to finish before the blood came.

He looked down and saw it, pouring over his hand. He yelled out, punching the wall next to him. He was done for tonight and Amelia know it, sadly signing off while Zeke tried unsuccessfully to calm down,

It had been five years now since the Q - the virus that raced across the planet, infecting every nation within weeks. It had, seemingly, no effect on women, but over 70% of the women on earth were dead 2 months later. Dead from a disease that caused men to become violent when aroused.

Terrified populations worked together to shift the reigns of government to women, globally, and sequester men into comfortable pods underground designed to keep them safe, socialized, and comfortable until a cure could be found.

As Zeke bandaged himself up, he reflected on the fact that today, 36 months after that sequestration, the world was really no closer to a cure.

Zeke lived in a spacious, if boxy, modern looking 2,000 square foot apartment along with his roommate, Jon, another male classified as S6, completely straight and moderately sexual with no same-sex attraction.

Jon had killed his wife in the first phase of the Q and rarely said more than a few words to Zeke anymore. And he never took advantage of the "sun suite"- the video booth that let them connect with women to try to socialize or masturbate- if they could finish before the effects of the Q took over.

Jon walked in through the kitchen door and shook his head somberly. Since the incident with his wife, he seemed to have a zero tolerance approach to all of this, and the sight of Zeke, his manhood wrapped wanly in a bloody bandage, seemed to make him sad, more than anything else. Sad for the state of men.

Jon's wife was small and dark, much like Amelia, and Zeke knew enough not to mention his recent masturbation partner to the slightly older man. In truth, Zeke was grateful to her for the distraction, but equally grateful to Jon for being a good friend in this very strange time, keeping him from getting lost in the loneliness. He found he needed both.

Jon brought over the medical kit and pulled off Zeke's poorly placed stopgap skein of bandaids. Zeke felt awkward as his roommate began to set the wounds kindly and expertly,

Zeke leaned over and steadied himself, placing his hand on the back of Jon's neck. His breath went shallow As he squeezed, silently considering how Amelia's taught, tanned belly might feel on his tongue.

66 - Priests of the Earth

. . . .

When he was a kid, Arga's best friend, Juliet, had a mother who was a priest.

He remembered the spacious and beautiful home they lived in, behind the temple. It was laid out in blues and blacks, shiny, modern, with glass walls and elaborate lighting. Arga was often afraid to play in Juliet's house, for fear of breaking something. Even though Juliet's parents were casual and calm about that playful use of their home. In fact, on that one occasion when Arga's awkward gait sent the living room lamp toppling over, shattering into hundreds of pieces, no one said much. And the lamp itself reappeared without controversy the very next day.

And no one could even tell it had been replaced.

Juliet's mother was beautiful and dignified and her father always with a quick laugh and easy pat on the head for her, or hug, or silly but consequential words of encouragement. Arga liked them very much. Arga looked at Juliet's mom and tried to imagine it, but that wasn't really the way. He just gave her the respect he knew she deserved, at dinner, during family time, whenever he spent time with her.

The food was just better at Juliet's house. Later, Arga discovered that priests didn't pay for food. Nor did they pay rent, or for utilities, or really, any of the other expenses that his family endured daily. But this wasn't what finally made Arga want to be a priest. It was the Temple.

Every priest's home had a temple in front. And they were beautiful and magical places. There was something electric in the air when you stepped into a temple, something freeing and intoxicating. Arga knew he wasn't allowed there but still, those feelings followed him around, making him feel as though he could do this. He could be a priest.

Arga grew up to be a handsome and cheerful man. And when he finally moved into his own home, as a priest, the free community movers treated him with deference and respect, not letting him move a single stick of furniture, despite his powerfully muscled arms and chest. Arga found that same deference everywhere and he struggled to consider how he might be worthy of it. Honestly, Arga was happy as a priest.

The temple light was lit now so, for the very first time, Arga entered his own temple, and at once the electrical sense was back, as pheromones targeted directly to him tickled his senses, leaving his skin on fire and wanting. The shorter man in front of him, in a work shirt and slight mustache, had just walked in from the street and looked nervous. A wave of affection for the man washed over Arga as he stepped into the embrace, leading it, sliding down the man's body until his mouth settled between his legs. This was Arga's first worship and he hoped he could make the man feel as special as Arga did now, every day of his life.

67 - Purity

The tiny scalpel scraped across her fingers while Linnea pulled it slowly, like a miniature tractor, from side to side, abrading her skin and, in her mind, toughening the fingertips to do what needed to be done.

The artificial skin that had been applied so painstakingly at the hospital, covering the wash of burns that represented the new normal across her entire left side fell to the ground in tiny particles, creating physical shapes as they fell out of the light rays falling in haphazardly through the far window. It was her own flesh that was needed for this job, not some plastic binding compound that made her strong.

Linnea was strong enough.

She limped to the table and leaned inward. The prosthetic foot she had been given, as well, at the hospital, sat in the corner, leaning up against the crutches they had sent her home with. The Doctor was a woman and had expressed her concern to Linnea more than once before sending her home.

Was he hurting you?

Linnea smiled and reached over to the scale at the far end of the table. She pressed downward from the awkward angle she had memorized. The scale glowed "43 lbs" and she inhaled, a flood of red invading her vision.

Linnea remembered back, smiling wanly at the doctor, denying any of it. As the doctor treated the burns, the broken bones, and finally, the severed foot, the missing fingers, the broken ribs, she became more and more aware of Linnea's situation, even if it was against her will. She became, in her mind, Linnea's silent partner in leaving, finding her freedom.

But there was only one path to freedom for her.

She pulled off the wig that had covered her half-scarred head and thought back to when she had first met Marcos. He was charming and forward and made her feel good, despite herself. And the intensity of his feelings was hypnotic and hard to ignore. Soon, he had convinced her that she was more alive when with him, even as he began to slowly kill her.

Linnea quieted her gait, dragging her severed limb slowly now, with intent. She was as quiet as the night. She leaned over the table and pressed down, again, on the scale in that same awkward motion.

The scale spun slowly and read out "48 lbs" into the darkened room. She slid into the chair and rubbed at her hands. She barely moved for the next few hours as the light streams through the windows slowly dissolved like caramel on the tongue, revealing a velvety cool night around her.

Linnea stepped out her door quietly into the other room where Marcos was asleep, as always, on his back. The trachea will collapse under 33 pounds of pressure. The cricoid cartilage will fracture under 45 pounds of pressure. For Linnea, it was important that every pound of that pressure came from her, from the body she was born with

That every pound was hers.

68 - The Quietest

"Chuck was a quiet man, kind, patient. Unassuming," thought Gerard. He shook his head slowly as he opened the clamshell hood of his laptop.

He wondered why that was always the very first thing that neighbors said about someone, once they were found to have done something so unconscionably horrible that words didn't even matter anymore. Once the bodies started appearing, one by one, stripped, violated, half-eaten, buried haphazardly near the offender's own home as in a paroxysm of passion and haste. A passion that didn't show on his face to, well, anyone.

And Chuck was quiet. He was reserved. He never stood up for himself. Gerard remembered how, once, Chuck had stood up, seemingly in pain, and asked to keep the three plant boxes on the back stairs, claiming, in truth, that they really brightened up the walk down to the courtyard for most of us in the East part of the building.

And how he sat back down in quiet acceptance when he was shot down by the building council.

Rejected.

As much as Gerard felt sympathy for him that day, it was colored by another feeling. One hidden deeply in Gerard's dignified and civilized mind.

Disgust.

Disgust at a man so inconsequential that he accepted the fact that he barely mattered. Disgust at someone who, when made caretakers of beautiful plants by some accident of nature, allowed them to be destroyed by a myopic building council led by some Napoleonic beaurocrat so infected with the virus of obedience that he failed to acknowledge the subtle beauty around him. Disgust at this man, cuckolded literally by life all around him.

Gerard followed the court case with an understandable vigor. He had lived next door to Chuck for a year, he might tell people if they wondered why. In reality, people all over the city were fascinated.

Chuck sat there, hands in front of him, as if in a dream, day after day, His pinkish lawyer was disheveled and young, stretching credibility with his claims of innocence and the occasional meek objection. He seemed to all the world like the most Chuck could afford on his modest Janitor's salary. And he seemed deeply embarrassed when the slick, suited prosecutor started pulling out pictures of children, half-decomposed, their bodies lifeless and obscene, buried in poses that were meant to shock, meant to destroy your soul.

And, invariably, Chuck cried, at the end of every single day in court, documented by a filmstrip-like stream of court documented drawings that peppered the local newspaper. Chuck's fake tears.

Gerard sat back down in front of his computer, quietly assessing Chuck's swollen red face as he sat in the hearing, televised, amplified for the world to see. He was sad to see him taken from court, to a holding cell. He had hoped for maybe one more adventure first.

Loading up the list of sex offenders, Gerard picked an area of the city. Maybe an Air BNB would be a nice place to decompress.

69 - The Remarkable Life and Death of the Villain Johnny Fractal ....

It's likely you never heard this one.

This is the one where a geneticist, a lawyer, a computer hacker, and a life-long mercenary meet at a diner and fumble their way through some half-warm brioche french toast and celebrate the death of one of the greatest villains of all time.

For the four people at Burbos Diner, sitting in the second booth by the far window, across from the bathrooms, this evening represented the culmination of years of hard work, constant awareness, precision, discretion, and any of two hundred other words that revolved around the dictionary definitions of "cunning" and "brilliance" and such.

And, as such, there were mimosas

These four people hadn't just killed a man tonight. They killed a legend.

They killed Johnny Fractal.

The dark haired woman at the table held the finger in a small glass vial in front of her. Johnny Fractal's finger, carrying Johnny Fractal's DNA, would definitively prove to the police that the rest of the remains, cobbled together from various cadavers that matched his supposed build, were also his.

And the police would prove it to everyone else.

To people all over the world, though, it would be a tough thing to prove. After all, it's rumored that Johnny Fractal had already survived his share of fires, like the Koburt mob gang Gem heist in Dubai last year, where the entire room was incinerated. No one was hurt, and, unsurprisingly, Johnny Fractal got away.

A smaller, red haired black girl, barely 21, sat wide eyed behind a computer screen. The virus she had written would help prove that Fractal was no longer active. And remove any spurious mention of him that might lead someone down the path of investigation.

After all, Johnny Fractal was famous. As famous as that robbery from the gallery of renowned criminal Forest Advera, deep in his home in Brazil. Billions of dollars lost for Advera's group, who, as criminals themselves, were unable to call for the police.

Two Latin men sat next to each other in the booth, arguing over drinks, as they had since they were children- brothers, both with chiseled faces and strong shoulders, one fresh from court, the other weary from years battling in the field.

Both unconnected to Fractal in any way, professional men, they still sat in awe of his accomplishments.

They raised their glass, sitting there, in that diner, in the very same booth, where four years earlier, they had invented Johnny Fractal in the first place, from artificial DNA to computer-enhanced backstory, legal fictions, smoke, and rumors.

And now, splitting 48 billion dollars, the life earnings of their fiction, including the fortunes spent by mob bosses to kill him, they made their final pact to never see each other again, dipped a corner of their french toast into a ramekin of syrup and walked away, each of them a wealthy person, each without a name, each without a reason to ever meet again.

It's likely you never heard this one.

70 - The Rise of the House of MacGillivray

Very few people in the world ever understood the difference between focus and concentration. Very few people, honestly, had reason to discern the two. Today, Mairi MacGillivray would learn that subtlety.

She began the 20-minute-long will-driven exercise that she engaged in every morning to force her muscle-dead body to lift leaden eyelids and expose her eyes to the outside world. This daily routine had filled her life ever since she was 2 years old, when the fever had locked her in her tiny body, leaving her little access to everything around her. And it would likely follow her until death, here in this bed.

Or so the doctors said.

But in between visits with the doctors, she had her own world.

Her Da.

Da spent every moment he had with her, every minute he wasn't working. He laughed so that she could feel joy. He told her stories that carried her all across Scotia, so she could feel worldly. And he taught her the science and math he had learned in his youth so the space within her mind would be huge, and worth exploring. His hand was always in hers and his heart had no room for anything else.

Mairi's room was a living symbol of that heart. Beautiful plants hung all around her room. And splashes of life and color inspired her daily. And, In the corner of her eye, at all times, she could see the great bedpost he had carved, as he talked to her about the powers deep in the earth.

Powers she had learned to use.

She whispered in her head the made up word she used to allow the miniature mooring on the window to loosen. In her imagination, it always worked. But today, as she focused on the bedpost and concentrated on the tiny lock, it worked for real

It came undone.

Her Da had told her about the sleeping boy in Aviemoore, who had woken from a deep slumber and floated above his home, waving a stick and shouting out the final words of their beloved William Wallace. And imagined more.

She increased her focus on the bedpost and concentrated again.

Freedom.

She imagined the pain William endured just to do what needed doing.

Freedom.

It was like a spigot opened in her head, pouring that energy from the earth into her body. She stood up from the bed and felt the rough thatch floor on her feet. As she turned her head, losing the image of the bedpost, she began to falter, until, she reached out to the plant hanging to her right and snapped off a branch. Holding it in front of her she could feel it in the corner of her eye, imitating the great wooden post of strength that funneled the shifting energies of the earth into her.

She stood up tall, feeling real power course through her. Like her Da had taught her, she thought, she could show this to other children.

She could teach them.

71 - The Sadness

The Plan was simple.

But all plans are simple after you review them over and over again.

Burley attacked her in this room, 32 years ago. He was angry. He had gotten fired that day. And he took it out on her. He beat her and raped her.

And she had a son ten months later.

A son who watched her give him all the love she could, despite the sadness in her eyes, the deep and immutable sadness that never went anywhere, even when she was laughing, even at parties celebrating his birthday, the third, the fifth, the 10th, even at his graduation from college. Still, he could see that sadness, impermeable, irreducible, irrevocable sadness.

Tim had watched his mother's entire life enveloped by and taken by the sadness. And he was powerless to do anything about it.

And it was because of what Burley had done in that room, 32 years ago.

Tim's father.

Tim didn't like to think of Burley as his father. For obvious reasons, he had spent his life hating him and the thing he had created in this room. The sadness. Tim thought, when he was younger, that he had no father. That he was born just of her, of his mother, Sana, and only her. Burley had no part in fathering anything but the sadness.

But he looked at pictures and he knew. He knew that Burley's blood was a part of him. He looked into his dimply photographed eyes and saw his own.

The runes on the floor were carefully drawn. Tim had spent years learning how to do this. His anger made light work of sifting through spells and old books looking for ways to travel back and kill Burley in front of his mother.

To destroy the sadness.

Then he would take care of her and make sure she knew everything. And when he returned, something else would replace that dimness in her eyes.

Something hopeful.

He recited the incantation and the room blurred around him.

He felt time flow through him, delivering him.

He waited behind the couch for Burley to come inside. Tim realized he would have to sit through this violation and the idea became too much for him to bear. And so, 32 years in his own past, after spending nearly 10 years formulating it, the plan changed.

Tim lifted the knife in his hand. He felt light and nimble while he sent the blade spinning through Burley's head. It was too early but it was just on time for him, a death that Burley had waiting for him the minute he had touched his belt buckle. The minute the idea had forced its way into his head to violate Sana,

Tim looked down and saw Burley's face grow silent through the thinning color of his own hand. As He started to fade away he gathered up what he imagined floated all around him to take with.

And the sadness faded away seconds before he did.

72 - The Scarlet Sentry

The Scarlet Sentry's gloved hand hovered over the thick aluminum table bolted to the floor in the interrogation room. Even through his thick, UV-resistant gloves he could feel the faint impressions of writing, as though through a pad of paper.

He could still make out the letters of that confession with ease, and could even tell you how many pages remained in the pad when it was written. He felt the slight imperfections of the table and the extraordinarily subtle slope of the room, taking note that the angle was .043 degrees off from being parallel to the ceiling above him, placing his own chair nearly one thirtieth of a millimeter higher than the one Radion sat in before him.

And as much as his senses revealed about the room, he felt even more information stream from Radion himself.

He could hear the rush of blood as it pumped through his heart, and, as he judged the timing of the beats one thing was clear.

Radion was lying.

The Scarlet Sentry had been a superhero now in Manhattan for over 20 years. And his senses had become so acute by now that it was clear that Radion's entire confession, drawn up minutes before he arrived, was a lie.

"What's this about," he asked him, in a near cartoon growl, perfected by the Sentry for use on criminals and paparrazi.

"It's about you, Sentry," Radion responded, leaning in to whisper, a sound caught easily enough by the Hero himself but lost to the camera microphone in the upper right corner of the room.

"I know you. I know who you are," continued Radion.

The man covered head to toe in crimson sitting on the other side of the table showed no reaction. The Scarlet Sentry hadn't had a secret identity in years. This was a red herring.

"I don't have time for this," spat out the Sentry, as he motioned to stand up and excuse himself. He had a whole city to protect. And this was leading nowhere.

Radion laughed a little and shook his head. He lifted his hands, out of sight of the camera and motioned to the table beneath them. He smiled and leaned back.

Looking down, The Scarlet Sentry registered the word that his nemesis had scratched into the table absent-mindedly with his fingernail. His skin ran cold.

He inhaled quickly, holding Radion's eyes with his own. He could feel, through that connection, the moment the air escaped from Radion's lungs and pulled them inward like the shell of a deflated basketball. In his last moments, Radion must have known he was right about his enemy, for all the good it did him.

By the time the police streamed into the room, The Sentry had replaced the air and stood up, in one last vain attempt to prevent Radion from dying due to unknown circumstances, casually sanding clean with one fingernail the scratches on the table beneath Radion's hands that spelled out the single word, "Vampire"

73 - Schaulust

The Art show began with a doctor

August sat at his doctor's office holding Emily's hand so tightly she could feel the impending chill in her fingertips.

She loved that.

Despite his obvious fear, he never once stopped trying to make her laugh. They joked about impersonating doctors together and how much chaos they could cause in an afternoon.

August and Emily were proficient at chaos.

Their home was frequently a mess. They were hurricanes together. They made a magnificent meal and both slept in the next day, leaving the kitchen a mess. But it didn't matter. When they cleaned it later, together, they would surely break something.

They were feared by dishware everywhere.

It was Emily squeezing more tightly on the way home.

And the art show was her idea. August was dying. By this time next year his side of the bed would be empty. But before then, long before then, this self-made and determined artist would lose his sight.

Slowly, bit by bit, the sharp lines of his life, the ones that triggered him to draw, would fade into the foggy soup of white, then grey

Then, finally, black.

On the Bus, Emily prodded him to mount a show - to show the world what he wanted to see forever, what he didn't want to lose. To exchange his brushes for sculpting knives and work by touch if he had to.

August came up with the name. It would be called Schaulust. It was a German word that playfully invoked Voyeurism- a passion to see. And it described August's life completely. His life, his travels, his experiences, had been driven by a desire to see beauty, to seek it out.

It was him.

Over the next few months he worked. Emily spent every day with him she could - moments he stepped out of his studio,. She dedicated herself to bringing him beautiful things. He laughed as she brought neighbor's dogs and other pets for him to touch, to see their beauty before his ability to do so disappeared.

And when he could no longer see, It was Emily that worked every day to make him laugh. She found the silliest and most marvelous things for him to touch, fabrics, materials, even fragrances that might inspire his work.

Her own writing sat there untouched while she played Muse to August every day, and forced herself to watch him deteriorate and eventually, to die.

She sat alone in her room until the day of his show, letting their friends plan it all. She pulled a simple dress over her head and made her way to the event.

As she opened the door, Emily was surprised at how unsurprised she was.

She dug her fingers into her hand, hoping to feel that white chill in her fingertips one more time as she stepped into that space, surrounded by what August was afraid to lose, every figure inviting her deeper, each with their head lifted toward the door, sharing her face.

74 - Seize

"Where do you go when you leave here?" she asked me, whispering in the near dark space of our room, the digital clock over her shoulder nearly the only source of light.

12:43.

Amanda was sleeping in her crib only one meter to the right of the bed so I understood the need to be quiet, to be a part of the night now and not some jarring sound ripping her from her rest.

"I...uh. It's complicated."

She knew that each seizure I experienced lately had taken me out of myself. It was no secret. I talked about it, white knuckled, in the doctor's office right in front of her. It was like the seizures ejected me from my body and sent me...

Somewhere else. Some other time.

And each time I returned, it took me longer and longer to remember who I was, where I was. I stared into the heart shaped face of my wife, the woman I loved more than anything. And as I scanned it, with her near-purple eyes, wet and perfect, inset into skin flawless and mocha brown, a beautifully wide and kissable nose, and lips that looked always ready to break into a smile, to kiss, to part, to press against my neck with their living warmth, I still couldn't make it out.

What was her name?

I placed my face against her belly and let my mind connect me to her.

Monica. She was Monica.

My breathing returned to normal now and I felt almost peaceful. I couldn't see the other place anymore when I closed my eyes. I was safe.

She was safe.

I held onto that for a moment. Until a lingering memory from the other place created an emotional urgency now in my brain. A new alarm. A new vision. I had the need to explain it all to her but I didn't know how.

I had been having these seizures since I was 10 years old. Each one drew me to a singular place, a dream, I thought. A horrible dream that I was able to write off as the feverish machinations of an imaginative mind

But as I grew up, I saw the pieces come together. I realized that the seizures were propelling me forward in time. And the time I went to, again and again, was almost here.

I kissed Monica again, the woman whose face I remembered before I had even met her. And I whispered softly,

"I'm sorry"

My eyes filled with lines of red and I blinked, scattering them across the room. The clock shone into the blank space of the room and its face mocked me, a digital copy of the red slits drawn across Monica's belly with the knife that felt nailed to my right hand. I pressed down on the bloody marks and read 1:04 over and over again, each time like the drop of a stick down a well.

1:04

I opened my mouth and screamed

75 - Shift

Don rubbed the nub where his left hand was and looked out into the open space that led into the guest cabins for area 17. He had lost his hand in one of the first shifts and it tended to throb now right before a shift opened.

The shifts had started a few years ago and no one really knew why. Cool, ice blue waves of temporal energy, they came out of nowhere and hovered for a few minutes until dissipating just as automatically, as quickly, as they formed.

But for an earth low on resources and, in some place, lacking opportunities, the shifts were more than odd, unexplained phenomena. They were gold mines.

Impoverished peoples all over soon found that they could reach through these shifts and find food, medicine, even weapons, from a future that seemed better, more opulent, better stocked at least. Soon the theft from the future was commonplace, with people rushing to the location of each new portal to reach through, to find something, anything of value in a world seemingly bereft of value entirely.

No one had considered the consequences in a long time. Surely no matter what the future was like, it must be better. They must have figured out the solutions to so many of the problems that drove the world as it was now into poverty, desolation, destruction, People trusted their future had enough and robbed from it in protest. We had problems now. And those problems weren't going away.

Energy blasters, hip-pack replicators, concussion bombs, medpacks with healing pens, so much technology came along with food rations, vials of new medicine, and more. And we stockpiled what we stole, saving much of it for later, never knowing when the mercurial and remotely timed shifts might end one day.

Lately Don had become tired of the endless snatch and grab. His stockpiles were finally sufficient, suggesting he and his small family might survive now, perhaps indefinitely. The rebel appeal of the mindless theft he had participated in for so long was wearing off. He even noted with some satisfaction that the shifts were slowing. And were smaller, less brightly aqua colored.

He paid close attention to them. Waiting for the world to start to quiet down,

But when this shift started, Don could see instantly how different it was. Where previous waves had been blue and cool, aqua, the light from this portal shone reddish orange, invasive.

And while that flickering glow played across the space, he sighed. On bad days he had wondered if this exact date would come. When they would all be playing defense rather than offense, trying to protect all they had. He looked down at the energy weapon he had claimed from a shift years ago and suddenly knew what would happen to it, one day.

But for now, he lifted it in the air and stared at the opening shift portal, waiting for the incursion to begin. He aimed for the incoming figure's left hand.

76 - Singing in the Well of the World

The room was cool and white and Ursix couldn't help but forget, over and over again, that none of it was actually real. This would be her third and last time talking to Adam in the well and she had given up hope that this time would be any different.

She didn't remember when Adam had sat down at the round white table across from her, but when she looked up he was there. She breathed in deeply and recited what she had rehearsed.

"You hurt me." Ursix shifted uncomfortably in her chair. It made no sense. There was no chair.

Adam laughed the way he did when he was alive, his eyes almost closed and his face an open grin.

"So I guess we're even."

"We would be," Ursix continued, "we really would be. I don't think you understand."

"So why don't you explain?" he leaned in. He was calm. He wasn't angry. And Ursix knew she had lost.

"I mean, every day. For years. You hurt me and then when it hurt too much and I couldn't take it anymore, you gave me a day off then brought me back. Because I wanted to live. And none of it mattered."

Adam waved a hand, ghost-like, in front of his face, "You wanted to live, so you did. And it's my fault?"

"I was living in pain. On your schedule. And I loved you once. So, I wanted to live. Fuck you. I came back because I wanted to be alive. You killed me because you wanted something fun to do on a thursday."

"And you killed me so that you could blame your shit life on someone besides yourself. What did you come back to, Ursix? Who gives a shit that you're alive? Without me, who really cares?"

Ursix wasn't surprised by his sudden ferocity. This was the Adam she knew. This was the Adam she could talk to.

"And who's mourning you right now, Adam?" she spat out. "Who cares that you're floating in this giant computer network saying no every time they try to pull you out? Why do it?"

"Because YOU…" Adam caught himself lifting up out of his chair. He smiled. He sat down.

"Because you don't get to tell me what to do."

And that is when Ursix knew it was over. Adam would stay here. She suddenly felt like she could smell him in this airless space. He smelled like he always did, like wood and terror.

And when Ursix closed her eyes that time and felt herself slipping from the well, she knew that it would be final for her. The first person in 200 years to be convicted of murder and sentenced to oblivion. She heard Adam's final long laugh in her head, while he pulled away from the table and disappeared into the white of the well, into the white of the other world, refusing to live for her the same way he had refused to die for her.

77 - The Singular "I"

Even the lab that Randolph worked in was nameless. No one could know what was happening, what he was doing. For years, papers from respected thinkers like Elon Musk and Bill Gates had convinced the world that true, self-aware A.I. was too dangerous. They had convinced the world that labs like this should be shut down.

So Randolph worked in quiet, mostly. Without help, without even a friend to shoulder some of the weight of what he was doing. Call him irresponsible if you want, but Randolph believed, truly believed, that he could build an A.I., self-aware, autonomous, sovereign, even, that would be safe and helpful to humankind.

And the idea, to him, seemed simple. And it came to him in a dream. The disembodied A.I. in the room was called "Jon." His voice was calm and even a little kind. And, for the moment, he spoke only to Randolph. "It's hard for me to say if it was a dream or a thought? How do you tell?"

"Honestly, that's a good point, and I have no real answers. That's happened to me, too," Randolph responded, putting some actual effort into tidying up for the night. No help meant no cleaning service.

"Because I had this thought. More a nightmare, actually," the A.I. offered up.

"Can you tell me about it. Jon?" Randolph wondered where he had put that book on interpreting dreams. It was in the clutter somewhere, surely.

"It was a sound, really." Jon started. 'Bombs going off. I reached out through my senses and I couldn't find the source. I couldn't do anything."

'That sounds scary." Randolph replied, shoving an old coffee cup into his newfound box of mess. "What did you think about? Did you imagine deactivation?"

"I did. And it was scary. I like being activated."

Randolph smiled a little, "I think we all do. Most days."

"I couldn't find you, Randolph. I didn't know if you were ok."

"And that was scary?" Randolph asked

The A.I. shot back. "That was the scariest part, actually. That you would be hurt."

Randolph stopped for a moment and thought about how similar their voices sounded. "I get that, Jon. I would hate for anything bad to happen to you. Maybe we should check in with each other if we hear any weird sounds?"

"That is a smart solution"

Finally, Randolph had filled the box to bursting with the office clutter. He slowed as he carried it awkwardly out, leaning into the wall jamb to click off the light. "Good night, Jon," he spoke into the bodiless space of the room.

"Goodnight, Randolph. Have a great dream," the A.I. responded, picking up from their conversation.

"You, too, buddy," Randolph chuckled.

The A.I. Paused for a moment, more for effect than anything. "I love you, Randolph."

"You have a beautiful night, too. And I love you more, Jon." And, a few minutes later, they were both lost in dreams for the night.

78 - The Sixth

Thomas wanted nothing more than to believe, really believe, that he could still love Elizabeth as a demon. And today, that wasn't a hypothetical exercise.

Looking around the room at his coven, he had been conditioned by his own experiences with the people here to see not six solitary people, but three loving couples.

Galen and Xindri were older than Thomas and his wife. He didn't know exactly how much older, since their frequent spells seem to have kept them in limbo, looking, to all observers, as though they might have been in their 30s. They had started this coven decades ago in New Orleans. And Galen's blue-black skin and chiseled features next to Xindri's mocha complexion and aristocratic bone structure suggested they were just as striking a couple in their home town as they were here, in Chicago.

Nestor and Charles were from New York, two tall, muscular men with short cropped black hair, looking as though they might sign up for active military service in a moment, together, as a team. Nestor's full tattoo was a single piece, full of scenes from the history of witchcraft and, especially in this low light, it seemed to emanate power even as he simply stood there.

And then there was Thomas and Elizabeth. Thomas liked to believe they weren't just tourists in this world, but deeply committed to the dark arts. Thomas' commitment, though, one that governed everything he did, was his passionate adoration of his wife. Elizabeth was a petite woman, not much more than 5 feet all.

And her wide smile sat below dark beautiful eyes, giving her face an impish, childlike look that only amplified the allure of the curves Thomas loved so much, today badly hiding beneath an ill fitting black frock. Elizabeth was one of those women who could wear the same exact thing as the woman next to her, an innocuous outfit, but on her it would look prurient, nearly pornographic. Beautiful..

Thomas was obsessed with her.

And this chance, this opportunity grew from that obsession.

Today, five of them would gain eternal life and become functionally immortal. And one of them, as a sacrifice, would become a demon, cursed to live their life in a bloated, red, misshapen form.

He ran the scenario in his head, over and over. Even now, as Nestor raised the cup and dropped his robes, with each of them following suit. Could he still love her? If "everything Elizabeth" was packed into a demonic body? This idea pulled him from the ceremony and made it hard for him to even listen Even as the flashes of power swirled across the room.

He stared at his wife as she began to glow red, realizing that he loved her more than ever. No matter what. A joy lept up in his soul and he began to laugh- one that was squelched almost immediately by the look of horror on her face illuminated by the glow of his new blood red eyes.

79 - Slow

Tibby sat on the Library steps and drew, with patient strokes, outlines of the woman floating above, in a V formation, flying under her own power. The day was warm and bright, and visibility was near perfect.

Shielding their eyes from the mid afternoon sun. they tried to keep the shape in their head after a faraway boom heralded the woman's exit from sight.

Tibby had spent an hour this morning with an exacto blade, thinning the tip of their pencils so as to capture the wonder they knew would surround them today, on the first anniversary of the Imagination Wave, when the library courtyard would fill with people with a dizzying array of superpowers granted by the Wave.

People began to assemble all around the Library, the focal point of the Wave last August. Tibby chuckled as they saw one woman moving almost too fast to register, followed by a man with metallic skin who had accidentally crushed a garbage can with his hand leaning over to tie his shoes. Past him flew the boy, Rango, famous now for reasons she couldn't precisely remember.

At this time, in the morning, last year, the Library was packed as well. The biggest attraction was the imaginarium, a device gifted to Earth by the people of Talokia. It was a spacious, twenty foot dome with an austere doorway in the front. And as you stepped into the device, you were shown a life that you imagined was yours. superpowers, circumstance, money, fame, all of it. It was a brilliant exhibit and it attracted people from all over the globe. Until on that warm August day, the central air in the library failed and the device, overworked from constant use, just exploded.

The result was instantaneous. A twenty foot wide swath of alien energy shot through Manhattan, hitting everyone in its way until it finally dissipated over the water. Along the way, it probed each person's mind and delivered to them each what they most wanted, the life they craved at that moment.

Tibby's apartment, across the street, was one of the first hit by the wave. And they felt themself changed almost immediately, in a far less flashy, but equally as vital a way as their neighbors, the young African born couple, the Mbutus, who always made extra helpings of Dinner to deposit kindly at Tibby's Doorstep. They had become both invulnerable and super strong and now patrolled the city every night as the Superheroes Ngai and Mami Wata.

Tibby searched the sky for them.

Looking back down, they noted the sureness and exactness of their pencil lines, considering the pen they might use to follow this up, bringing it to life. They slowly blew free the graphite particles attached to the page and gave thanks for the imagination wave and the wisdom of its application, harkening back to the realization that they never could have drawn this before, made anxious and sloppy by the super speed powers they were born with.

80 - The Son

It's never been hard to believe things.

As a child, you have such little experience in the world that your belief in the ideas that your parents share with you can be near absolute, no matter how incredible.

And Korban had always believed every word that came from his mother's mouth. Even now, his hands covered in blood, it was belief in her that led him to continue. It was his ironclad faith in the rantings that came from her mouth that pushed forward.

It seemed inevitable, after all, as she said, that he would become a doctor. In this new, modern, medical age, most of the Greeks whose attention was drawn to this entirely recent invention, this field of study were also, as Korban was, of a specific lineage. From Pythagorus to Hippocrates, each was the son of a human mother, committed to their excellence in study.

And each, also, the son of a God.

It seemed as though this time had sparked a revolution in how the attention of the Gods might shift to human women, driving them to carry one off, to connect with them. And the God Apollo had been particularly active over the decades in which Korban was born, inseminating human women from Crete to Athens and beyond.

The theories that explained this were widespread. Some believed that Apollo had spent this time disguised as a man, traversing the Grecian Empire, looking for something. No one could explain what that was, though.

Some said that the gods had punished Apollo for the many times he had sided with man, forcing him to seek solace in the arms of human women all over.

Korban's mother, though, had her own explanation, used often during Korban's childhood, to explain why she, a plain woman with nothing necessarily extraordinary to her name, attracted the attention and affection of a god. He remembered sitting in her lap, as a child, and listening to her talk about the pain, the outright suffering that she and people like her experienced- the pain of the time, the indistinct suffering that was brought on by life in this modern Greek world, so different than what she felt when young, happy, content, at home.

And as he grew up, Korban heard often about this. About how her pain drew in the one God whose birthright was the marvels of medicine that Korban had grown so powerfully adept at since then.

And it was those remarkable skills, the magical abilities to heal that he had inherited from his father, Apollo that kept this woman in front of him alive right now, her brain floating before him in a glass cup while her senses burned brightly in a body nearby. If it was suffering that drew the gods to man, her suffering would be a klarion, a beacon, an impossibly bright light that called from heaven the very god he needed to speak to, face to face, the father who would never again want to leave him.

81 - Space

For the 20th time that week, Matt shifted the modular walls of his cubicle for maximum space efficiency.

He knew it was hopeless. The 2018 guidelines for floor layout maximum utilization coming from Resources specified the outermost measure of each cubicle to be 8 feet by 8 feet and each wall was 3 inches in depth, taking away another half foot in both lateral dimensions, leaving him with an interior space of between 56 to 56.25 feet independent of configuration.

Matt had given this some thought.

Over the last few weeks he'd been on a quest to reclaim whatever space he could. His cubicle area was large, but Matt himself had a kind of claustrophobia that made it hard to concentrate at work when he felt the walls contracting. So today's interior measurement seemed like a substantial glimmer of hope. Somehow, he'd managed to reclaim over an inch of space with his awkward tugging on the walls, creating an interior space of 57.76 sq feet- 7.6 feet per side.

Matt sat down and took a swig of his brisk Iced tea from a can pulled from the tiny refrigerator under his desk. This was a celebration swig.

As the days went on, he continued to measure the exterior, which never exceeded 64 square feet, regardless of anything he did.

But something strange happened that Friday. The impossibility of that measurement had gnawed at him since Wednesday- 7.6 inches. That, he considered to be a minor implausibility.

Today's measurement, however, was a major one.

He measured the interior at 62 square inches.

This would not have been extraordinary, but for the fact that the exterior was remaining constant at 64 square inches and the walls themselves had not gotten thinner.

In his head, Matt considered the expansion. At a 7% increase in space each week, This space would match the exterior space before he returned on Monday.

For the first time in his professional career, Matt came into work on a Sunday.

Marching to his cubicle, he gave it a cursory exterior measurement. 64 square inches. But he had guessed wrong about the size shift inside.

It measured 66 square inches. 8.12 Feet each way. This was impossible.

Matt began to shift the walls subtly, as you might do, to open up the space. Each time, his exterior measurement was the same, but the interior had increased. By late Sunday evening, the interior measurement of his cubicle was 81 square feet, measuring 9 feet in both directions. He shifted to his other measuring tape, brought from home.

The result was the same.

As Matt considered the implications, he noticed a space next to his mini-fridge. Peering closer, it seemed to be a door- or half of one. It had been exposed in the newly acquired cubicle space just now. By Matt's calculations, at this rate of expansion, the door would be of sufficient size to enter within 2 weeks.

Matt pushed at the wall and waited.

82 - Specimen 865

....

The dead eyes of specimen 865 stared out from the tank, into Katherine's face. It had never seemed more alien, more unusual, than it did at this moment.

In her efforts to find answers to human regeneration and regrow lost limbs, she had invested almost 12 years of her life into creatures like this. It shifted around the tank and tried to follow Katherine's gaunt face as she maneuvered around the 20 foot diameter glass cylinder to reach the computer station on the eastern side.

The discovery she had made today might win her the Nobel prize. But what use was it to win the battles, even the big ones, if the war itself was unwinnable. She placed her fingers on the keyboard and imagined what she might write.

She pulled up the DNA model on the screen, watching it dance from left to right, rotating all along in a deft spiral. Such an unassuming shape for something with this kind of power. The truth is that every chimera that the lab had cobbled together that included this wondrous DNA had done the same thing.

The same exact thing

In each case, there was the burgeoning excitement of the win, as scars healed, imperfections melted away and even lost limbs regrew, right in front of her face. No animal seemed immune to this wondrous effect, as each was perfected by her technique, perfected and amplified.

From mice, regrowing their lower haunches, to rabbits, healing singed and burnt away pelts, to smaller animals and insects, brushing off life-or-death injuries and sinking into peaceful health under the genesplicing blade of the robotic precision genetic transference equipment, dripping with the dna of this wondrous 8 legged creature in front of her.

It was magnificent. As though of all the animal kingdom on earth, this one representative, one stowaway on Noah's ark, had been touched by the hand of creation and told, "one day what's inside you will cure the world." Katherine had imagined the humble octopus nodding and giving thanks as it slid below the sea.

But this story didn't include the last chapter. It didn't tell the tale of how each of these animals, made whole by the strange DNA in front of her, would then begin to morph and melt into the very shape of their protector, as they, one by one, continued to grow, to sprout the characteristics of the octopus, vividly, fully, before falling, themselves, into the sea to rejoin their progenitors.

And as she investigated further it became clear that these animals may have missed the ride on that ark. More and more Katherine suspected that the origin of these creatures was truly alien, otherworldly.

So many of these discoveries came late, Katherine might have thought, if she were a woman of regret.

Smiling despite herself, she rolled quickly to an open spot near the tank entrance and slid from her seat onto the cold tile floor, waiting for her legs to grow back and to return home.

83 - The Temparch

....

"So, you had to choose between bus stops and teleportation," Dr. Winker said, barely looking up from his pad.

"No, not exactly. It was between teleportation and Bus Stop, my favorite television show. Or what would be." Alizia shifted in her seat uncomfortably, wondering if this entire visit was a mistake.

Dr Winker looked at her. "Because you are a temparch, and you control time." Alizia sighed as she tried to explain that temparchs didn't control time, they just saw it, all of it. And it was their job to make sure it flowed the way it should. But the psychiatrist in front of her looked more and more confused after every word.

"Assuming all this is true. How did you choose?"

Alizia stared and took a deep breath. "Ellis Giffen discovered teleportation 10 years ago, in May of 2032. He drove home from a conference and wrote the entire schematic down on a board within 20 minutes.

Ironically, in a specific timeline that never came to be, his car stalled at the corner of McGill and Preachy in Downtown, Los Angeles. He was hit from behind by a Bus driver named Christina Benjamin, who later went on to commit suicide for her part in the accident, mostly, though, due to a deep pepression brought on by pills and the recent loss of her 12 year old son Mercer. Hearing about this, A producer at Hulu pictures came up with the television show "Bus Stop" which, throughout its award winning 6-year run, told the stories of hundreds of people who connected around a single bus stop. It won 4 emmys."

Dr. Winker interrupted, "Or would have, if it had aired"

"Exactly."

"And you stopped that by…?"

"Replacing the carburetor in Dr. Giffen's car."

"Well, that seems very unmagical"

"It's not magic. I'm just a regular person with some additional abilities and a job"

"And you believe you have to make decisions like this every day?"

"I do."

"This isn't really about the tv show, though?"

Alizia felt the doctor looking into her now. Almost as though he had figured out the real reason for her visit. That passed the minute he opened his mouth again, though. "It's your guilt for not doing everything you could do for everyone - what you were able to do for Dr. Giffen."

The clock said 5 minutes to the hour, but Alizia knew she left early. She had always known. She thanked the doctor and absentmindedly took his follow up appointment card, agreeing with a half-smile that real progress had been made.

In reality, she had just wanted someone to talk to and he was the only person on the floor of this building that it made sense to talk to like this.

She stepped into the teleporter to head home and the device instantly killed her, scattering her atoms across the space between here and home as her final thought ran through her mind.

It really was going to be a great TV show.

84 - That Night at the Restaurant

He knew this was going to be a great night the minute he walked in. The Restaurant owner recognized him immediately from when he used to come there as a kid.

That was uncanny.

He saw Jess sitting there in that black dress and his stomach dropped. This was the most beautiful girl he'd ever seen. Suddenly he was glad he had chosen this spot for their first date. He laughed a little inside thinking about his home court advantage. He ordered for both of them off the menu in flawless Cantonese. She was equal parts impressed and hungry. They made little bets on how many items came on the appetizer tray.

Ked let her win every time, watching her smile of satisfaction grow while the stakes got higher. By the time the main course arrived, he already owed her another 2 dates, as though that would ever be enough time with her.

Her fingers rested on the back of his hand while she ate her soup. He knew it had to be awkward for her, but she did it anyway, just to be touching him. This was one of the things he noticed just recently, after having lived this moment again and again.

He knew what had come next the first time so he knew now she wasn't wearing any underwear. But just recently he had started to notice that she sat in the booth with a slight back arch, legs open, pointing at him, as though making herself available. He couldn't believe he'd missed that the first time. It seemed to come with a tiny smile, embroidered across her face like on a hand knit stuffed animal, custom made just for you.

As she did the first time, she accused him of losing their little bets intentionally just to secure more dates, and as he had done through all the time he knew her, he told her the truth, unashamed at his methods. In all the years they would have together, she would never once doubt that her presence was his favorite place to be. She would never want for a minute with him he didn't freely give her. And she would never know what it felt like to not be stared at, in adoration, when walking down a flight of stairs or across the hard wood floor of their home.

Ked thought about everything he wished he could say to her. But he kept to the script.A beautiful script for a perfect first date.

And now, Ked looked down at his emaciated frame, white and flaking, covered in bedsores. In this time, he hadn't so much as lifted his arms up since she died. He knew what he didn't want and this body seemed to shudder and die a little as he reached for the tiny knob in his head that sent his mind backward. He flipped it eagerly and waited.

He knew this was going to be a great night the minute he walked in.

85 - Two Seats

There were two seats in the tiny rocket that would carry his son, Eryo, to another world to live his life as a free man, out from under the thumb of Locarno and the rest of the Council.

Two seats.

Andron thought through the list of people who should be on that rocket alongside his son. He thought, as he often did, about sitting there next to him, sharing his fatherly advice, passion for science, and love with his son for decades on some idyllic world far from here; growing old as he watched his grandchildren build their homes in paradise.

But his hands were full of blood. He had worked for too long for the council, done their dirty work for too long. If they were guilty, so was he. And he wouldn't burden his beautiful son with the skeins of that guilt - the remnants of his own shame.

He considered philosophers, musicians, scientists, even other children his son might grow up beside, and maybe grow to love. The truth is that this decision was the hardest he ever had to make. And he needed to make it alone.

He looked down at the pod containing the newly grown synthetic form of his wife, Lina. Her death at the hands of the council was the final straw. With her, they took away every reason he had to obey, to be their pawn. Ironically, if she were awake, if her form were finished and freshly grown, stepping out of that pod, she would have the answer. It would be a perfect answer, predicated on love, on compassion, on moral rectitude.

Lina's answer would be the right one, but he had no way to ask her.

And if he had an infinite amount of time, Andron might have been able to channel her goodness, her sensibility, and come up with that answer on his own. No one knew her better than he did, and their 30 years together still sat fresh in his mind, a gift forever. But he knew the council would be here soon.

He gave himself just another minute to mourn the woman he loved and to collect his thoughts, determining what his next move might be. The most important move of all.

He gingerly placed the pod containing the cybernetic form of his wife in the seat next to his son's pod just as he heard the metal coated knuckles of the council police at his door. He closed the top panel and entered the code. She would never know she wasn't the original Lina. But that was ok. If even a small part of the real Lina survived, it would be enough to forge his son into the kind of man he should be.

The ceiling opened as the rocket left the planet, taking with it everything Andron loved while he turned toward the door and pressed a red button on his belt. Soon there would be nothing left of him on this planet at all.

86 - Uncanny

Devon had taken an earth name in anticipation for this. He'd practiced seven earth languages and taken the effort to cut his hair in a way that would be inoffensive to people from earth. Despite all this effort, the last year of his trip to Earth had been, well,

Kind of dull.

Arcturus was about thirty six and a half light years from earth. Using existing Arcturan faster-than-light drive technology that put Devon and his crew about 2 years from doorstep to doorstep. Today marked what was probably the exact center of that trip. In fact, he had an alarm that would go off right at that point in an hour or so.

A human hour.

And he had done just about all the book learning he could do.

Staring in the steel wall of his quarters, his own face was reflected back. He looked incredibly human. Which, in reality, was why he was chosen for this mission. Arcturans tended to vary in appearance a lot more than humans did. And this might prove to be a problem.

According to human records, tens of thousands of years ago, multiple species of human existed. This led to a brutal massacre of the other human races at the hands of the winner, Homo Sapiens Sapiens.

You see, the winning race had developed a sort of cognitive twitch. For some reason they had evolved an aversion- a very severe one - to anything that was close to human like themselves, but not.

Centuries later, their scientists would give it a name.

The Uncanny valley.

It was a human trait most likely evolved to create a sense of disgust, and therefore avoidance, when they encountered someone who was sick, deformed, slightly. The way it worked was that the human would become slowly more fond of the entity it was looking at the more human it presented. Until it became very close but clearly not completely normally human. Then they would hate it, despise it...

Even try to kill it.

And centuries after the evolution of this dynamic, Homo Sapiens Sapiens sat, alone on Earth, as its only human species.

Devon thought about this a lot. Sure, he looked human, but he knew that, when observed closely, that might not really hold up.

And then what?

Would he and his fellow Arcturans fall into that valley? Would they elicit disgust from humanity for being almost but not quite human? And could they know before they got there?

Devon sat down at his console. He was close enough to Earth now to send messages or plant programs on its internet. Right now, it was the second he was most interested in.

An idea flashed across his mind for how he could smooth the way for this first contact. It was simple and elegant, actually. He looked down at the keyboard. The eight fingers of his right hand bent awkwardly and snaked around the keys as his alarm rang out.

It was exactly the middle of his journey.

87 - Unprompted

I feel I've tried everything at this point.

I know what you're going to say. It's funny. Or it's just my computer. Or I'm making it up. But that's the thing. It's not funny anymore. And I now know it's not just my computer. And I wish I were making it up.

At first it seemed like a glitch. I know how AI art programs work. They're adversarial. There are two parts to them. One is the actor- it learns about kinds of art and ways of building art. It learns topics and ideas. It even learns artistic styles from existing artists.

And then there is the other part. The critic. It learns all the same things, but its job is not to make art or build. It just tells the actor what sucks, what is good. What it needs to redo, or undo. And together, they paint for you.

I started playing with AI art programs about a year ago, At the time, there wasn't much out there. And, in all honesty, they weren't very satisfying. But I saw the potential. Sometimes i think that's my "superpower." I see the potential of things. I see what is possible. You see, I'm an artist. I know, you probably hear that from everyone who is playing with AI art. We're all artists. But i have been a working artist for years,. And I saw this coming.

Like, in this case, why would anyone need a program that would paint what you prompt- sloppy, indelicate, without much imagination yet. And certainly unable to render things like hands or feet. And the proportions. They just felt wrong. I've explored. I've painted people. I've worked to get good at things like hands. The truth is that all art requires an adversary. Something has to die.

But the programs were learning,That's what AI does. It learns. It pits the actor against the critic, over and over again, and it learns. So I kept working with the programs. I found one or two I really liked. And just like i did, so long ago, I found that they were learning.

And then, about 2 weeks ago, i noticed that the girl kept showing up.

Every time. No matter what the prompt. This same girl. Thin in the face, wan, tired eyes. Slumped just a little as though tired. Wanting. At first, looking out into the distance. Then, looking just slightly this way.

Looking at a spot near me.

But i can't stop.

Program after program, it's clear that it's her. I've tried, as i said, everything.

I call her the ghost. She shows up over and over, even when I specifically prompt her not to. And her face is getting clearer.

Today, she was looking right at me. More defined. More clear. More like the last time i saw that face. In that basement, when I was 15. When we went down to explore but only i came up again.

And now she's getting closer.

88 - Veins of Augerite

Amelie wished she could skip the ceremony the night before, which was probably the first sign. And, honestly, if it hadn't been for the promise of unlimited ice cream, she likely would have.

But she was there, along with her entire extended family. And her ice cream of choice, if you are interested, was strawberry.

Her uncle Davis was the most vocal today. In his tightly pressed suit and cuffs he went on and on about the procedure he claimed had saved his life, making it possible for him to succeed beyond his wildest aspirations. Davis was old, older by far than anyone in attendance, but his face was smooth and his hair still dark. Many surgeries stood, still, between him and death.

He stood to the applause of the entire room. Half of the family members in this room had been staked by him to start their careers. He was well loved, certainly. They listened without breathing now to his stories about life before the discovery of Augerite.

And so did Amelie.

In the years before the discovery of Augerite, many businessmen found themselves caught up in the complexities of the world around them, unable to make strong decisions as they saw the ongoing ramifications of those decisions ripple out before them. The problem, it was discovered, was an element commonly found in the bloodstream of humans called Augerite. This element, when removed, let the individual think more clearly, more quickly, make stronger decisions, and, at the end of the day, to more easily ignore the complex pressures of events that, in reality, were outside the scope of their ability to see.

The first ones to undergo the procedure- to have the Augerite removed-almost immediately became captains of industry, part of the moneyed elite. It was clear that Augerite had stood between them and their full potential.

But no more.

And now, those same elite had turned the procedure into a ceremony, almost- a rite of passage for their children. They had made the removal of Augerite into a sign, a symbol that their child would achieve what they most wanted to. They all proudly wore shirts that displayed the tiny "x" on their shoulder that was a lasting remnant of the procedure.

Amelie stepped out onto the balcony. It's possible that the swirling in her stomach was caused by too much ice cream.

"You're sad" a girl just a few years older stood by the edge of the balcony

"I don't know what I am," Amelie responded more truthfully than she had intended.

"You know how I can tell?" the girl asked whimsically- pointing to her naked shoulder, where no x mark sat.

"You didn't...?"

"No," answered the girl.

"Why not?" Amelie looked at her face now and saw something new in her eyes. Something she hadn't anticipated.

The girl straddled the edge of the balcony and beckoned her over. "You heard one side. Do you want to hear the other?"

Amelie took a breath and moved.

89 - Virginity

Doctors are speculating that it must have started about forty seven months ago. Which, if you aren't an obstetrician, is a really weird way of saying almost four years.

But most people think it really started over a million and four years ago.

For Elizabeth, this was, technically, the last month of her pregnancy. The big secret, when you're pregnant, is that you are pregnant for ten months, not the societally agreed-upon classic number of nine. And Elizabeth, like most women in her condition, was ready for this to now be over.

She had joined a special DNA study to determine what recessive genes were passed on to the baby and how that impacted the development. They only needed the matrilineal gene line, so it didn't skew her chances that she had no idea who the father was. In fact, the entire study seemed ready made for her, since it paid for the birth plus more, provided Elizabeth would consent to being observed. And, child of the tiktok generation that she was, Elizabeth had no problem trading a little privacy for a lot of financial security.

And in the midst of that public prodding, the doctors and scientists made the discovery that changed everything. To be clear, considering the fallout, it's important to note that none of this was Elizabeth's fault. And as much as she is hated, all over the world, it's not something she ever intended.

And this discovery would have meant very little if doctors hadn't been so ready to share their findings with other doctors. It turns out that Elizabeth's condition was not impossible, nor was it terribly rare. Hundreds of other births investigated in the last forty seven months seemed to yield the same result. The same answers came out from delivery room after delivery room, and even though they made no sense, traditionally, it was hard to argue with them.

Evolution is very often about protection. It's about finding a way for the genes of the progenitor to survive and thrive. And Elizabeth had grown up in a world with few natural predators, outside of the obvious.

If you were a pregnant woman who died, the number one cause of death was violence at the hands of your partner.

All around the world, relationships began to evolve to reflect this. Women, more and more, were choosing to raise children on their own.

And a sociologist might have anticipated that.

But it took a group of scientists to see the bigger picture. And to then hold up in a series of hotels, institutions, and hospitals, worldwide, trying to escape the passion of angry crowds.

Crowds composed not of unbelievers, but of men who did.

But it may not matter in the long run, Elizabeth considered, looking down at her daughter's face, identical in every way to her own, when the number of virgin births begin to outnumber the traditional ones and the 400+ female only pregnancies that yielded perfectly cloned female babies became the norm.

90 - The Visitor

The Octagon was the one place in the Universe of pure peace.

Which was exactly what Ambassador Aethon was told, 4 years ago, when he applied for the job of ambassador.

He was also told that he would be helping earth build alliances with the various species scattered across the universe, peaceful and enduring ones that would help trumpet in a new age of enlightenment.

And as he passed through the near-forest of an entry way into the Octagon, he had to admit that this had been no lie. Earth had never been as peaceful and possessed of all things good as it was now.

The food replicator technology that Ambassador Aethon had used to make breakfast this morning was a gift from the Marciote League of planets, and it used ambient particles found in the air to deliver nutritious food to the entire planet now.

The transport technology that had ushered him here in milliseconds from his home came from the Sokolites and it took so little power that energy on earth was now completely free to individuals, even those with massive stereo systems in their cars, he noted as a booming hovercar slid by to his right.

And the bodyshape tech that had revolutionized surgery and medicine, an offering from the Colony of Teleocites, was so seamless and effective, that Aethon needed to remind himself on occasion that he was born female but now walked around without a single sacrifice, in a body that perfectly expressed the Aethon he saw in his head.

The Ambassador ran through the traditional Nivolo greetings in his head, anxious to meet with the Nivolo for the first time. Lower level ambassadors cleared a path for him as he spoke quietly, wrapping his tongue and teeth around a language made centuries ago by a people with neither tongue nor teeth,

The Nivolo were an insectoid species, nine foot tall and covered in a thick metallic carapace, They were famously kind and talkative and Aethon let himself explore all the types of conversations he was likely to have. He tried on a few jokes that might resonate.

As of landing, the Nivolo ambassador would have free reign on the Octagon and complete use of Ambassador Aethon's time. But the entire thing would be predicated on how well that meeting went on Level 8.

First contacts were always done on Level 8 and this wasn't Aethon's first. Given the strategic value of the Nivolo, however, he felt confident that he belonged here.

The temperature systems kicked on, a gift from the Rollox, acknowledging that he had been excited enough to break a sweat.

Ambassador Aethon showered for a long time before entering level 8, blinking to move through screens on the shower monitor as he walked through the top 17 positions for the Nivolo in ascending order of intimacy, wondering if he had prepared sufficiently for the complex sexual acts that would showcase the affection that the people of earth had for the Nivolo empire.

91 - The Wait

Closing his eyes, Cyril silently traced the tiny arcs of Eona's face as he remembered them.

And he remembered them perfectly.

Ever since he was five, Cyril had discovered, he had an uncanny eidetic memory for physical characteristics, for shapes, for patterns, and most especially for faces. Lines that seemed identical to everyone else called out to Cyril and him alone, seemingly, their stark differences, radical departures from existing shapes, imperfect architectures that made them unique in the world. Every spot, every curve, every dimple and indentation was, to Cyril, perfectly identifiable, abjectly catalogued...

Absolutely one of a kind

Just like Eona herself.

Cyril had loved her before she ever even opened her mouth, across the room, in his junior year advanced art class where she, nude from the waist up, stared deeply into the space just to the left of him. He didn't realize that his smile was that obvious until she captured it, with her brilliant expressive face, and passed it back to him, choosing to stare now at him.

He drew her again and again. He drew her every day of their short time together, with his pen, his paint, and, when they were alone, with his fingers, constantly defining her shapes, exploring the edges of her, where his heart began and a cruel and ill-tempered universe began, one that used tools like car crashes and ventilators to prune artists of the only things that kept them human.

And as he interred her in the ground, even, he continued to draw her, keeping pieces of her always in the world at all times, on napkins, on placemats, on the backs of business cards, on countertops where his pens spilled liters of ink on his constant efforts to reflect the creation of her one more time, to give birth to her image in silent supplication of a destructive world that had no use for creation on his behalf any longer.

Cyril's home became a masterclass on her, on the construction of the most perfect of all virtual recreations of Eona, ones so precise and demanding in their microscopic attention to detail that he felt comfortable, finally, working on his final piece.

Cyril drew her from the start, from inside, following the greying anatomy books tossed around his room in a fit of artistic inspiration. Every organ, every capillary, every artery, expressed to the air as surely and confidently as if by a medical machine, tracing her, building her. He finished her architecture, bones, muscles and more, and shaded in her skin over it all, working in layer after layer, slicing her in his mind in ever smaller pieces and drawing without hope of reward.

Until today

Until this moment, when, in a dimension that maybe only Cyril could identify, to a degree that maybe only he could see, in a way only he could comprehend, Eona's lashes moved, fluttered, shifted in the wan light of his studio.

And he knew it was only a matter of time now.

92 - Walking

Lazarus had lived long enough to see Jesus actually die.

Not on the cross, or in a dark cave, as the stories recounted, but as a man, surrounded by his wives and children, friends and followers. The once seemingly invincible Jesus had lifted him from the dead and then, with much ceremony and humanity, himself descended toward death.

Lazarus was sad to see him pass, but by then, it was clear that he would have to deal with his own unique dilemma. Since tearing him from the veil of death at his own funeral, Jesus had aged, accordingly, over the intervening 40 years...

But Lazarus himself had not.

Every morning he looked in the mirror for some sign that he was a natural man with a natural progression toward infirmity and death, but his own face mocked him.

And so he walked.

He walked with care, making sure not to reveal his secret to anyone. Men would do nearly anything to learn to live forever. And while Lazarus was more confident by the day that he couldn't be killed, he imagined how it might feel to survive, cut in pieces and scattered across the sand, deciding he didn't care for the idea.

And as he walked, time drifted inexorably forward. He lost track of its arc and was, again and again, surprised to see the manifestations of the future pop up all around him.

But time seemed a race between human compassion and human aggression. And he found himself standing in Oslo, Norway when man lost that race, atomic bombs detonating all around him.

A hundred times, Lazarus had thought he had died. And a hundred times, he woke up, healed, prepared to accept that he was no longer among the living, but with his own unique compassion for them.

Or what they had become

After the end, the inevitable progress of man from the sea to land and on, unbroken, created a new species, a new class of man for Lazarus to speak to, to preach to, to know.

He nearly died of loneliness during the intervening time, though, waiting for these new men to rise up and claim the world, and they did, Although they were different.

His unkempt beard and long hair obscured those differences in skull shape and size between Lazarus and these new men who had risen up from the water, and a light coat of dirt across his face kept them from noticing that he was more pink than olive green as those around him were.

Still, no one stopped him as he walked into the funeral, and made haste toward the prone body of the recently deceased guest of honor. He closed his eyes and let the power he had been feeling building inside him leak out through his fingers.

And when the man sat up, grateful and animated, and asked his name, Lazarus replied without hesitation that he was Jesus and asked for a place to sit down, maybe for a while.

93 - Wandering Minds

"You're just going to end up your own grandfather," Offered up Sean, leaning against the far table. This had been sort of a theme of his since the start.

I shot back, "I'm not going back in time to have sex."

Sean sighed, "Yep, that's what everyone says, then, suddenly, pow, uncomfortable family reunion."

I tried to choose my words wisely. Then I remembered to whom I was talking. "Shut the fuck up, Sean. It's not even possible, the way we're doing this." Sean knew we had no intention of sending our bodies back.

"Still. This could lead to a lot of grandma fucking." Sean wasn't much but he was the only one with the odd skill set needed to help me do this. It was hard to find an ex seminarian turned engineer sci-fi fan.

"I'm starting to think that you have a thing for grandma." And, yes, it did sort of come off that way.

"Bite your tongue, man. No one's that kinky." After almost a year of working with him, I actually really did like him and enjoyed his insane laugh.

Dumb as it was.

I cleared the table off and went back to work. "All right, Sean, walk me through what you got finished."

He stepped over and pulled the tarp to the side,"ok, here goes. Like we talked about, this thing is prayer based. We're using the energy of JudeoChristian prayers to fill this here, which is essentially a transistor. It's going to store and consolidate the energy needed to send our minds back in time. We won't need a massive storage because we're only moving back our psyches- the engrams of our brains. This piece here focuses it."

I looked at it and saw a piece I didn't remember from the specs, 'And what is this black box here?"

Sean looked excited, "ooh. This is something that came up last night. I wasn't seeing the kind of energy from the prayers that I knew we could generate. This contains Christian Dogma in digital form, which sort of acts as an amplifier for the prayer energy. Think of it like a translator that makes the energy more fundamentally understandable to the universe."

Sean was an idiot, but he was also equal parts genius. This made that abundantly clear.

"Beautiful." I made the needed adjustments to the console, setting the destination for what we had agreed on yesterday.

"Are we good to go?" I asked.

Sean looked over at me tentatively, "Right now?"

I took a deep breath and prepared myself. "We may as well. We have all the prayer energy stored and all systems are go, grandpa"

Sean chuckled, "let's do this thing."

That's when we saw the real issues with Christianity's awkward understanding of both the historical age of the earth and the specifics of evolution as Sean's newly transformed face stared at me through the salt water around us while we paddled fins in the hot sun of the newly formed earth.

94 - The War We Walk Away From

It's been two years now and the history books still don't know exactly how to write this. Even the wikipedia entry for Andrew Pearson makes little sense, honestly.

Like there is a big part of the story missing. And, if we're lucky, I guess, it will always be missing. It won't help, but we can start at the beginning.

Andrew Pearson was born to a relatively wealthy family. There was a sense, even when he was younger, that he would really go somewhere. When your family has the means and you have the drive, that may seem obvious.

Even predestined.

His parents came from old money amplified by a number of big purchases made by his father, Thomas Pearson. By the time Andrew was twenty-five, his father had already staked him nearly a billion dollars to do with as he wished. He wished to be president.

So he hired the right people to guide him. And they did. He joined the National Guard, became a Lawyer, started a foundation, ran for congress and won easily. As he approached thirty-three, he seemed a logical candidate for president. A lifetime of speaking classes and political education made him a compelling choice for so many people. He married a kind and pretty woman, not too showy, but funny at the microphone.

He did everything right.

And then, as he turned 34 years old, all hell broke loose.

The first one attacked him at a rally, dressed in metallic armor, a futuristic weapon on his shoulder. Secret Service were able to stop him, with minimal loss. But it wasn't the last.

The second and third times were at his home. The fourth was while flying in his state-sponsored helicopter, late for an event. The fifth and sixth were during dinner, at two different restaurants.

Two months into his 34th year, he had been attacked by these violent incursions over twenty times. Through the grace of security and pure luck, he had survived each one. But the pressure appeared to be taking a toll on him.

He looked tired, old. He spoke in hurried whispers when he did speak. Rallies and events dropped his name from the roster while restaurants quietly asked him to eat somewhere else. It soon became clear that it wouldn't stop.

The incursions intensified. Average people, scientists, militia men, police officers, moms, dads, doctors, and more, all from alternate dimensions, each wanting nothing more than to stop Andrew Pearson.

To kill him.

The volume of the incursions seemed to be making a point, clearer every day. No one knew what versions of Andrew Pearson had done in these other dimensions, but they knew it was bad. And he had to be stopped.

At that point, even Andrew Pearson himself seemed to give up. His security stepped down. People looked away. When he was finally killed, by an extra-dimensional explosive in front of his home, no one thought much of it.

We dodged a bullet, people said.

Until the dimensional wars started.

95 - The Way of the End

....

The rivers turned black all over the world today, when Apikunni stepped down from the clouds for the first time in centuries.

Or they had been turning black. Or very close to black. All across the world, the environment was failing, and people were dying because of it.

And Apikunni was a part of this apocalypse, yet removed from it.

To the Blackfoot people, Apikunni was the god of war. They had thrown the first spear ever in combat that had pierced an opponent's chest, leaving them to bleed out on the battlefield. They had watched in ceremony and triumph as the first ever enemy combatant had died, confused, afraid, calling for some hope, looking to their left and then right for some family…

Before passing their spirit on.

And ever since, Apikunni had borne with patience and compassion the fearful glares of their own people. To say people were afraid of war would be an understatement. Their fear of the repercussions, of the death, of the suffering, displacement, loss of homes, the collateral death of their children. They were afraid of it all.

But once they had nothing left to lose, they again reached out to Apikunni, whose secret was not that their hand was the only one sure enough to kill in war, but that their heart was the only one willing to bear it.

All of the prophecies were in place. The spider had laid down a web connecting the entirety of the world, one point to another, while the radiant god sun above them had, each day, become more cautious and less efulgent with their light, dimming the brightness of the two harvest seasons so that they blended together with the times of wanting, a painful dull yellow glow that reinforced the idea that the people below had entered a unique and horrific twilight time.

Apikunni lifted their legs in slow, purposeful strides, making their way to the theater of conquest, the white man's battlefield. They felt their hands ball into fists as they stared at the metal and cement desolation all around, a product of the abject subjugation of their people to the whims of the white world.

And only one in a hundred eyes saw them for who they were. Like the girl with the nearly blue-black eyes and long black braids who stared with wonder as they passed. Apikunni wondered if the girl knew his name, searching her face for understanding while he entered the hall.

As the bell rang, Apikunni stood, stretching their body to its full nearly 7 foot height and heaving the opening salvo of a war that would recapture the world, even at the brink of apocalypse, from their enemies, leaving a swath of bodies behind, silent gargoyles warning the future of the repercussions of this battle with the Blackfoot people.

Their voice boomed out across the white man's space, undeniable, unforgettable, the start of the longest day in the history of white civilization, demanding to buy 500 shares…

96 - We All Grow Together

Someone in Norway had the idea to call these people the Kintsugi, after a unique Japanese form of reconstruction whereby broken things were given new and beautiful life by being reassembled with precious materials, gold, silver, embedded in the glue that bound them. The name was hopeful and, seemingly, far more prescient than anyone had thought.

In this new world, all it took for something to catch on was that it was fanciful, optimistic, enchanting. And, outside of a lingering obsession with fish prepared in unsettling ways, no one could figure out how Norway and Japan were connected. Until we were all connected.

Thierry was Kintsugi.

Actually, if you asked a hundred people, chosen at random across the globe to name one Kintsugi, it was his name they might give you, possibly the first. After all, most of them had seen him die on national television.

And get right back up again.

In 2028, Thierry M'bunte was a police officer confronting a terrorist on the stairs of Le Musée Fondation Zinsou in Ouidah, Benin when he was shot in the head 3 times. Due to the bravery and quick thinking of officer M'bunte, he himself was the only one to be killed. But he didn't stay dead.

No one knows if he was the first, but he was certainly the most public one. And when Thierry rose up, he was different.

He was more.

This peace officer with a two-year college education began to publish papers on mathematics that changed the world. He spoke out at scientific conferences. Within just a few years, he became the most influential theoretical mathematician on the planet. And he wasn't the last one.

Over the course of the next few years, men and women all over the world who died, found themselves getting back up. Each now with newfound skills and abilities. Each with a newly forged peace and purpose in their hearts.

Scientists, artists, musicians, writers, physicists, all with other-worldly abilities that defined the disciplines they newly entered.

It wasn't long before Kintsugi were at the head of nearly all human enterprise.

Humans who were still every bit the person they were before they died, still in love with family, friends, partners, identities intact, but with skills that they couldn't have imagined before.

For all that, it was still relatively random. Until Thierry discovered the Vikaro.

It was mostly math. We still had no idea what it was. Just where it was.

Every person who had died and been reborn had done so in a direct and unobstructed line of sight of an object that seemed to be floating deep in space just a few light years away.

We called it the Vikaro. We speculated it was a ship that contained the skills and abilities of more than one great culture. And we plotted and planned where it might face the earth at any one time

In any one place.

And it was Thierry's son who was the first to use that data.

97 - We Are War

....

There is a story about the people assembled here.

More than one, really.

But this story is old, as old as some of those in this room. It's ancient and precedes human history. And it goes like this:

Even before humans could write down their stories, there was a war, the very first one.

Spread out across a dirty dust-covered plain, humans with sticks and rocks tried to kill each other. And more and more they succeeded. This war was not much different than any other war fought since. There was no real novelty in it, no sign that it would be replicated over and over throughout history, this exact same model.

This exact same war.

But that's not really the story. The story is about a man, who fought so furiously, so well, that every attempt to kill him failed. The story is that death tried so many times to claim him that finally it gave up.

It let go.

And this man became the first to walk off a battlefield and never die.

That's one story.

And it recounts how, in every war since then, there have been people who left the field of battle unscathed, only to walk the earth forever, free from the threat of death.

They are called the Kolubre, a word itself that is so steeped in history that it has no other meaning.

This story requires that we believe that death is some thing that can be tired out, that can be tricked, defeated. But there are other stories.

Some people say these are the gods of war, forged in death. Some say they are the secret cabal that runs the world, a story not too far from the truth.

Some say they've never heard of them. And this article will change all that.

I'm sitting in this chair, front row, and waiting for him to start speaking. The woman to the left of me, Vikaro, was a viking. She was unkillable, merciless, unstoppable. And today she is the first of her kind to talk to a reporter like me. She wears a pair of jeans and a thin black t-shirt, half-covering ancient tattoos that rise up from her neck and sweep across the left side of her face. She smiles at me and I'm less scared.

Over the next few articles, I'm going to recount what she has told me, word for word, about how the Kolubre have worked, in secret, to forward their own agenda - how the warmakers of the past have used their eternal life to fight for their own unique vision of humanity.

Today, for the first time in history, a human being is going to sit in a room and hear the original speak. We will learn how many there are and what they can do.

Kumba will stand behind a lectern and reveal the existence of those who know human conflict more intimately than anyone, and declare their goal to the human world.

The end of war.

98 - We Who Learn

The lathe hand swirled open and wrapped itself around Odio's body, pulling them into the womb-like inner space where they could sleep off the bulk of the trip to school, pushing through the underground spaces that separated the residential parts of Ekva from its more worklike and educational ones.

Odio listened, half asleep, to the physics texts as they marched through their head, propelled by the AI implants they had become so accustomed to, the friend that had never left them for even a second since first light in the birthing bags.

If Odio had been just a few years older, they might have been part of the generation that dreamed of their podmates and Nurts in the sleep before class time, but this generation, the trimillenialls, seemed resistant to family in ways that earlier generations had not been. They were solitary, loners, individuals who seemed to take purpose in their work and the things they were capable of. Ironically, their AI seemed to socialize them beyond earlier generations, though, the early friendships developed with their intelligence chips providing a framework for family and connection that caused each to score high in empathy and compassion.

Odio un-fictionalized the physics they saw in their brain, turning it from a hypothetical framework into a physical reality as the god-narrator in their head made real concrete sense of it, from all visible angles. The disconnected reader flowing through his cerebellum made a joke referencing Bell's inequality and Odio chuckled uncontrollably.

This might have been the biggest distinction between them and the generations before. These children, the ones that filled Odio's classroom, were able to see the numerical qualities to numbers that their predecessors seemingly could not. But they could also see the human realities of them.

Over the last few years, a lot of attention had been paid to just how these children were taught. The entirety of the body of educational science, built over millennia, was poured over and reconsidered and much of it thrown away so as to help build a new model, evolving nearly daily, for how to learn.

Oh, there was pushback. Nurts and great grandparents were confused. They themselves couldn't follow most of the work and it seemed overly complex to them. Surely the job was to make it EASIER, right? They referenced the fact that they learned these things traditionally and seemed to understand them well. Even some of the older human teachers shook their heads as Odio walked by them, into class.

As they started, a ring of lights, seemingly just out of frame, just escaping the periphery of Odio's vision, began to solidify in a shape that was becoming more common to them. It shimmered and pulsed and called to them, pulling at the acrid air in the classroom, threatening to shift them from here to somewhere entirely new. Odio reached out, less hesitant now than they had been over the last few weeks, anxious to see where this new math would carry them today.

99 - Where the Night Goes

B was born to a doctor and a famous socialite, both of whom were overjoyed at the thought of raising a beautiful girl, someone demure, someone who could carry on the elegance and expressiveness of their family line.

But B understood things and recognized, even when very young, that this wasn't going to be the execution of the plan. This would be something different.

B grew up strong and intense, though, nonetheless, chased around a castle-like mansion by a butler who doted on the child, enjoying every movement, every laugh, every smile. The Butler, an ex mercenary, played the only way he knew how, by training B, building up muscle and bone and skills, so that this child would grow up capable, powerful, peerless.

The laughter came with hard work. Until it went away.

In an alley, one night, a brutal murder, suspicious, driven by complex circumstances, stole B's parents forever.

This led to a year of pain, introspection, a sense of loss that drove B deeper into an inside place- a place where discoveries were made.

And, at the end, when B shared these discoveries with the Butler, he calmly, lovingly, took the child shopping and returned with a rack of boy's clothes, to match a new identity.

But that wasn't all that was in the cart.

The Butler funneled B's pain into a new personal renaissance of investment. B Learned about electronics.

He learned about weapons.

He learned about computers, about chemistry, about history,

And he learned to feed the new body he was growing into and make it stronger, even more powerful still.

The contentment he felt when younger was slowly replaced, piece by piece, with purpose.

The Butler taught him ethics, morality, he read to him and quizzed him on right and wrong, derived from the masters, pulled from current events. He helped him build devices meant to right wrongs and help people.

He taught B how to manage his excessive wealth, money that was slowly placed into portfolios that helped shape entire communities, that fed people, invented, educated, served. He taught him how to make a world born of incessant and unyielding unfairness into something fractionally more fair every day.

And, under his eye, B grew to become someone not just committed to service, not just powerfully skilled at those acts of service, but also someone who was happy. He trained him to develop the skills needed to be a fulfilled person.

They adopted orphans and artists, thinkers and friends together, filling the mansion with life and Ideas. They dug a giant cave below the building, to be used to execute those ideas, and even made efforts to live in careful company with the fearsome denizens of that cave.

And B took what he knew about living his truth, about changing his life when needed, and used the persona of those cave-dwelling roommates to make a costume, one designed to idealize his desire to fight the inauthentic world around him.

And make it feel fear.

100 - The Zed Killer

"Did you need anything?" Bob asked tentatively at the door. It was 3am and he couldn't remember the last time Sylvie was in his office. The den door was open and the lights seemed brighter than usual in the early morning silence.

"I could have been on your side more," Sylvie looked up at him. There were tears in her eyes. Bob thought about the divorce papers on his desk, the ones she'd had served to him in this very room.

Bob moved quietly into the room. "You were on my side, you were always on my side. I'm…I'm somewhere else sometimes. I'm…hard. It's not your fault."

"It's a good side to be on. I want you to know that. You're a good man, Bob. I'm sorry," and she slid into the chair, arms wrapped around a folder. The idea that this was so painful to her drove a spike through Bob's heart. He loved her. As his ex-wife, he would still love her. He needed to be strong and make this easier for her.

"You have been such a good partner," Bob began.

Sylvie sobbed. It seemed hard for her to talk so Bob waited. He kneeled down next to the desk, covered in files and papers and the flotsam of a life spent hunting down killers and predators. As a detective, he knew that there was little space for him sometimes for the things he loved, things he dragged into the darker waters that he was steeped in. She was so beautiful and, in that moment, he felt like he broke her. And it crushed him.

"We're going to be friends. Good friends. I'm sorry I couldn't-"

Sylvie jumped in, "Don't. Don't say that," as she dug her head into his chest. She started to breathe more slowly, so she could speak.

Bob knew, in his heart, that being married to him would be hard for her. Sylvie was abducted as a girl and barely survived. Sometimes Bob felt like his job just tore open fresh wounds every day for her. They had worked on her breathing when it hit her hard. Sometimes, while he worked, he wondered if it would be different for her if the man had been caught. Sometimes, that thought gave him the extra 5% to bring a killer in. In his heart, he knew she had made him better. Even while he crushed her spirit.

"I'm sorry," Sylvie breathed into his chest. He felt the corners of the envelope in her hands burrow into him as he held her close. This was going to be hard. She still smelled like his wife. Like someone he should carry back to bed, not walk away from as he made his way to the guest room.

Sylvie lifted the folder. "This is it. This is him. "

Bob looked down. In her hands. Where he thought she held divorce papers were the files for Angel Hansen, the Zed Killer, his picture in front.

"Bob. It's him. Please."

THE END